Is That a Sick Cat In Your Backpack?

To Harris

Happy New Year

Is That a Sick Cat In Your Backpack?

by Todd Strasser

SCHOLASTIC INC.

NEW YORK TORONTO LONDON AUCKLAND SYDNEY
MEXICO CITY NEW DELHI HONG KONG BUENOS AIRES

ISBN-13: 978-0-439-77695-0
ISBN-10: 0-439-77695-3

Text copyright © 2007 by Todd Strasser

12 11 10 9 8 7 6 5 4 3 2 1   7 8 9 10 11 12/0

Printed in the U.S.A.
First Scholastic printing, January 2007

To Greg and Jen,
who don't have a cat
— T. S.

ACKNOWLEDGMENTS

Even though the Tardy Boys series is currently only two books long, making it THE SHORTEST SERIES EVER, the author will be forever thankful to the nourishing support of the many people who helped him through the difficult and hungry months during which this book was written. Without their daily input, the author would not have had the strength or energy to complete this work. Therefore he would like to thank the following people: Sara Lee, Mrs. Fields, Ben and Jerry, Dr Pepper, Colonel Sanders, Betty Crocker, Mike and Ike, the Three Musketeers, Aunt Jemima, Little Caesars, and Catherine Zeta-Jones.

AUTHOR'S NOTE AND WARNING

Dear Reader,

Congratulations! You have just begun the second book in the brand-spanking-new Tardy Boys series. You could say it's their "latest" book. Ha! Ha!

WARNING

Children between the ages of three and seven may find this book strange, frightening, and bizarre.

Children younger than three won't care one way or the other because their brains are like warm Jell-O and all they want is food and clean diapers. If you give this book to a child younger than three, he or she will probably eat it.

Children over the age of seven but under the age of ten might find this book strange and bizarre. But they probably won't find it frightening because they should know by now that Alien Space Cat Mind Control only exists in books like this and, sometimes, in the school psychologist's office.

Children above the age of ten but under the age of thirteen won't be bothered by this book because they are no longer children. They are now preteens. Sometimes preteens are called tweens. And some tweens wear jeans priced beyond their means. But that is another story.

Sincerely,

The Author

P.S. The first book in this series was called Is That a Dead Dog in Your Locker? But it wasn't really about a dead dog. At the end of that book is a postscript where the author refers to the Meowians from the Planet Meow in the Feline Galaxy. Since then, the Meowians have changed their name and the name of their planet.

THE MISSING CAT MYSTERY

To: Catmander Claw on Planet Hiss
in the Feline Galaxy
From: Cat Spy Scratchy on Planet Earth
in the Milky Way Galaxy

Sir, I have good news. I have landed
on Planet Earth in the Milky Way
Galaxy. The air is breathable.
There's lots of milk and water to
drink and plenty of small animals

like birds and mice to chase.

I will send more information soon.

After the big party at their good friend Daisy Peduncle's house, the Tardy Boys walked home. It was winter and, in the cold dark air, their breath came out in white clouds of vapor.

"Wow, winter came really fast this year," young TJ Tardy said through chattering teeth.

"'I'll say," said Wade Tardy.

"No, you didn't," observed Wade's fraternal twin brother, Leyton Tardy. "TJ said it."

Wade had dark, unruly hair and was thin and scrawny. He was not very good-looking but, if you drilled a tiny orifice into his skull, you would see that it was packed full of brain cells. His brother Leyton was blond and handsome and had broad shoulders and big muscles. But his skull was so empty that monkeys could swing from the branches of the trees inside.

"'I'll say' is just another way of saying I agree," said Wade.

"Then why didn't you say 'I agree'?" asked Leyton.

Wade rolled his eyes and sighed. It was no use explaining. Instead he said, "That note from our parents has me worried. If they've been kidnapped by aliens, there's no telling when they might return to Earth. What if they're not back by the time we go to college? How will we go?"

"I bet Mr. Roy would drive us," said Leyton.

Wade felt a shiver. Sometimes his brother was so thick it was scary. "That's not what I meant, Leyton. I meant, how will we *pay* for college?"

"Is college very expensive?" asked TJ.

"Yes," said Wade. "And that means the only way I'll be able to go is by getting a scholarship."

"What about me?" asked Leyton. "Can I get a scholarship to college, too?"

Wade doubted that anyone with as much open space in his skull as Leyton could get a scholarship. But he didn't have the heart to say this to his brother. "Yes, you can get one, too."

"How?" asked Leyton.

Wade knew that the best way to get a scholarship was to be TOTALLY BEYOND EXCELLENT on a school sports team. But this wouldn't be easy because The School

With No Name was also The School With No Sports Teams. That left the second-best way to get a scholarship.

"We'll have to improve our vocabularies," Wade said. "By learning the meanings of words."

"That sounds like a good idea," said TJ. "If we'd known what the word *toiletry* meant, I wouldn't have spent so much time trying to plant a tree in a toilet."

"And I'd understand why people park their cars in driveways and drive their cars on parkways," said Leyton.

Wade scowled. Leyton often said things that made no sense. But now Wade had another problem.

"According to the note our parents sent us, we have a cat," Wade said as he and his brothers went up the front walk to their house. In the dark, they could see the shadows of the broken bicycles, smashed skateboards, bent Razor scooters, partly burned sofas, and broken toilets that littered their front yard.

"But none of us have ever seen this cat," said Leyton. "So where could it be?"

"Maybe it's in the attic," said TJ as they went into the house and turned on the lights.

"I doubt it," said Wade. "If there was a cat up there, we'd hear it moving around."

"Then maybe it's in the basement," said Leyton.

Wade groaned. "Our house doesn't have a basement."

"Maybe it does and we don't know it," said Leyton.

"We've been living in this house all our lives," Wade said. "I think we'd know if we had a basement."

"Wait," said TJ. "Maybe Leyton's right. If we have a cat we don't know about, why can't we have a basement we don't know about?"

"That's it!" Leyton gasped. "The cat must be in the basement!"

By now, Wade was completely fed up. "That is the stupidest thing you've ever said."

Leyton hated when his brother told him he was stupid. Their friend Daisy said he wasn't stupid. He just had a different way of looking at things. "You think you're so smart," he grumbled. "But you don't know everything about everything."

"Be quiet!" TJ said as they entered the kitchen.

"Why?" Wade asked.

"Listen," said TJ.

Wade listened. "I didn't hear anything."

TJ pressed a finger to his lips. "Shhhh!"

"I still don't hear anything," said Wade.

"Neither do I," said Leyton. "Why did you tell us to be quiet, TJ?"

"I thought if we were quiet we might hear something," said TJ.

"Right," scoffed Wade. "We might hear the cat we've never seen in the basement we don't have. Guys, I hate to tell you this, but even if we had a cat we didn't know about, by now it's probably run away."

"I still think we should look for it," said Leyton.

"Be my guest," Wade said with a shrug.

Leyton frowned. "How can I be your guest if I already live here?"

"Forget it," Wade muttered. "Go look for the stupid cat."

While his brothers looked for the cat,

Wade sat down at the kitchen table with a dictionary and began to study vocabulary. Ms. Fitt, his favorite teacher, had told him that the more words he learned, the smarter he would become. And the smarter he became, the more chances he had of getting a scholarship in case he went to college before the alien kidnappers returned his parents to Earth.

Wade had just gotten to the word *aardvark* when Leyton rushed into the kitchen with a cardboard box. TJ hurried in behind him. Leyton shouted, "Look what I found!"

"A cat?" Wade was amazed.

"No." Leyton reached into the box and pulled out a black telephone. "A phone!"

"I didn't know we had a phone," said TJ.

"Didn't you ever wonder why we never

got any phone calls?" Leyton asked him. "Come on, let's plug it in."

"Why?" asked Wade.

"Maybe somebody will call us," said Leyton.

"Are you crazy?" Wade asked. "We probably don't even have phone service. I've never seen a phone bill. We don't even know what our phone number is."

"You never know," Leyton said, and plugged the phone in.

Briinnnnng! It immediately started to ring.

SLIME ICE

To: Catmander Claw on Planet Hiss in
the Feline Galaxy

From: Cat Spy Scratchy on Planet Earth
in the Milky Way Galaxy

More good news, sir. Planet Earth is
populated by many species of cats
like us. I will use direct-hypnotic
staring— which I learned from the
Hypno Aliens on Planet Hocus in

the Pocus Galaxy—to take control
of them.

In their kitchen, the Tardy Boys stared
in wonder at the ringing telephone.

"It must be a wrong number," said
Wade.

"What should we do?" Leyton asked.

"Here's a brainstorm," said Wade. "Try
answering it!"

Briinnnnng! The telephone kept ringing.
TJ finally picked it up. "Hello? Yes? No.
Yes. No. Yes? Okay. 'Bye." He hung up.

"Who was it?" Wade asked.

"Someone," said TJ.

"Who?" asked Leyton.

"I don't know," said TJ.

"Was it a man or woman?" asked Wade.

"Couldn't tell," said TJ.

"What'd they say?" Leyton asked.

"They found our cat," said TJ.

A few minutes later, the doorbell rang. The Tardy Boys hurried to the front hall and opened the door. Outside stood a person wearing a puffy white coat. It was hard to tell if it was a man or a woman because he/she wore a fuzzy white hat pulled down on his/her head and a white scarf wrapped around his/her face. They couldn't see his/her eyes because he/she was wearing sunglasses.

The person in white held out an old, tattered green canvas backpack with a peace sign stitched on it.

"Is this the cat?" asked Wade as he took the backpack.

The person in white didn't answer.

"Where did you find it?" TJ asked.

Without saying a word, the person in white turned away and walked past the yard littered with broken bicycles, smashed skateboards, burned sofas, and broken toilets.

Leyton closed the front door.

"Kind of strange to be wearing sunglasses in the middle of the night," said TJ while Wade opened the tattered backpack. Lying at the bottom was a skinny, scruffy gray tabby cat. It was missing patches of fur and had one ear partially torn off.

"This is one sorry-looking kitty," Leyton said.

"How do we know it's really ours?" asked TJ.

Wade reached into the bag and lifted out the skinny, scruffy animal. It lay limply in his hands. On its collar was an identification tag that said:

TARDY FAMILY
15 LANDMARK DRIVE
SOMEWHERE, USA
PLANET EARTH
THE SOLAR SYSTEM
MILKY WAY GALAXY

On the other side of the tag was a diagram of a planet in a solar system in a galaxy.

"Looks a lot like Al-Ian's Alien Return Dog Tags," Leyton said. Al-Ian was their friend and a brainiac who had believed in UFOs even before the Tardy Boys learned that their parents had been kidnapped by alien abductors.

"Or, in this case, a cat tag," said TJ.

Suddenly, a loud roaring sound came from outside, and the floor under the Tardy Boys' feet shook.

"What was that?" Leyton asked after the shaking stopped.

"Felt like a small earthquake," said TJ.

"That's weird," said Wade. "We've never had an earthquake around here before." He looked at the cat's identification tag again. "There's no phone number."

"Does it have a name?" asked TJ.

"No," said Wade.

"Then what should we call it?" asked Leyton.

"Skinny Kitty," suggested TJ.

"What are we going to do with him?" Leyton asked.

"The note from Mom and Dad said we're supposed to feed him," said Wade.

"Feed him what?" Leyton asked. "There's hardly anything here for us to eat."

"Know what cats love for breakfast?" TJ asked. "Mice Krispies."

Wade rolled his eyes. "Tomorrow after school, we'll go to the store and get some cat food."

But the next morning when the Tardy Boys woke up, nearly six feet of fresh white snow had fallen. The snow was so deep that it covered the first-floor windows and blocked the front door. The Tardy Boys stayed in their house all weekend. By Monday morning, the plows had cleared the streets and some sidewalks, but the snowdrifts were as tall as mountains.

Well . . . small mountains, anyway.

The Tardy Boys were getting ready for school when the doorbell rang. Outside was their good friend Daisy Peduncle.

Daisy was wearing a long gray coat and boots made of brown animal skins. Daisy's parents were hippies, and Daisy was their peace-and-love child.

"Are those boots made from animals?" Leyton asked.

"Yes," Daisy answered as she stepped into the Tardy Boys' house and shook out her long, braided brown hair.

"I thought you were against killing animals," said Wade.

"They're made from roadkill," Daisy explained.

"What's roadkill?" asked Leyton.

"Roadkill is a poor, defenseless animal that has been run over by cars and trucks," Daisy explained.

"Then those boots are probably made mostly of frogs and not many cats," said Leyton.

Wade made a face. "What are you talking about?"

"Because cats have nine lives, while frogs croak every night," Leyton said.

"Ha!" Daisy laughed. "That's funny, Leyton."

Leyton crossed his arms and smiled at his brother as if to say, "See? I'm not so dumb."

"Speaking of cats," Daisy said. "Did you ever find yours?"

Wade and Leyton stared at each other in surprise. Wade had been so busy studying vocabulary all weekend and Leyton had been so busy doing nothing that they'd forgotten about Skinny Kitty!

"TJ!" Wade yelled toward the kitchen. "Is the cat still there?"

"Yes," TJ called back. "He's in the backpack on the kitchen table just where you left him."

"Bring him here so Daisy can see him," said Wade.

TJ appeared in t he front hall with the old green backpack. He opened it and Daisy looked in.

"Oh, my gosh!" Daisy gasped in horror. "He looks so skinny and sickly!"

"After school today, we're going to the store to get some cat food," said Leyton.

"Oh, no, you can't give this cat regular old cat food," Daisy said. "He's much too thin and sick. This cat needs special food."

"Where can we get that?" Wade asked.

"You'll have to go to RePete's Cat Palace," said Daisy.

"RePete's?" said Leyton.

"You'll have to go to RePete's," said Daisy.

"RePete's?" said TJ.

"You'll have to go to —" said Daisy.

"Stop!" Wade cried. "We understand. We'll go to RePete's and get special cat food."

A few minutes later, they left for school. The snow was so deep that it covered the sidewalks and the only place they could walk was in the street. Icicles hung from bare tree branches and glistened in the sun. The sky was blue and cloudless.

As they turned a corner, TJ slipped and fell. Daisy, Wade, and Leyton did, too. TJ tried to get back up but slipped again. The same thing happened when the others tried to stand. The street was covered by a thin layer of glistening, yucky-smelling ice. No matter how many times they tried to get up, their feet slid out from under them.

"There's something strange about this ice," Wade said on his hands and knees. "It's much more slippery than normal ice."

"It feels slimy," said Daisy.

"And it smells gross," added Leyton.

"That's because it's not regular ice," a voice suddenly said. Coming toward them was their friend Al-Ian Konspiracy. He was wearing a puffy blue jacket and hood. Unlike the others, he had no trouble walking on the superslippery ice.

"Why aren't you falling, too?" asked Daisy.

Al-Ian gestured to the pointed metal spikes strapped to the bottoms of his shoes. "I'm wearing crampons so that I can run away in case alien abductors try to kidnap me. They also help when you're trying to walk on slime ice."

"What's slime ice?" asked TJ.

"It's what happens when Barton Slugg's trail of slime freezes," said Al-Ian.

"Is this slime ice?" Wade asked.

Al-Ian sniffed the ice. It smelled sharp and bitter and burned the inside of his nose. "Yes, I believe it is."

"But why would his slime ice be here?" asked Leyton.

Phoomp! Wham! Before Al-Ian could answer, a perfectly round white snowball smashed into the back of Leyton's head.

"Ow!" Leyton cried.

Phoomp! Wham! A perfectly round white snowball smashed into Wade's stomach.

"Uhn!" grunted Wade.

Phoomp! Wham! A perfectly round white snowball hit Daisy in the leg.

"We're under attack!" she cried.

HERBAL SODIUM PENTOTHAL

To: Cat Spy Scratchy on Planet Earth
in the Milky Way Galaxy
From: Catmander Claw on Planet Hiss
in the Feline Galaxy

Excellent work, Cat Spy Scratchy. We
here on Planet Hiss are very excited
by the news about Planet Earth.
However, we need more information.
What are the dangers? Are there any

animals on Earth that might stop us from taking over? What about the species called humans?

The perfectly round snowballs kept smashing into Daisy and the Tardy Boys. No matter how hard they tried, they couldn't get a grip on the slimy ice. Al-Ian moved back until he was out of range of the snowballs.

"Al-Ian!" Wade cried. "Can you see where the snowballs are coming from?"

"Up there!" Al-Ian pointed at a huge pile of snow beside the street.

Suddenly, the attack stopped. Wade and the others looked up. Standing on top of the huge pile of snow was Barton Slugg, the Tardy Boys' WORST

ARCH-ENEMY EVER! On Barton's shoulder was something that looked like a huge Super Soaker water gun. Only the barrel was as wide as a bazooka.

"What's that?" TJ asked.

"A Super Slammer snowball gun," Barton announced.

"Why are you firing it at us?" asked Daisy.

"Because you cheated in the great Toe Cheese versus French Cheese Debate," Barton yelled. "We were supposed to debate something about American history. But you stuffed the debate jar with stupid cheesy topics."

"If they were stupid, why did Ms. Fitt let us debate them?" Leyton asked.

"Because Principal Stratemeyer was sitting in the back of the room, and she had no choice," Barton said.

"You're the one who tried to cheat by using Fibby Mandible as an expert witness," Daisy said.

Instead of answering, Barton aimed the Super Slammer snowball gun and fired.

Phoomp! Phoomp! Phoomp!

Wham! Wham! Wham! More snowballs slammed into the Tardy Boys and Daisy.

"Stop!" Leyton cried.

"Are you going to keep making fun of my smelly feet?" Barton asked.

"Uh . . . can we think about it?" Wade asked.

Phoomp! Phoomp! Phoomp!

Wham! Wham! Wham! Barton's answer was a barrage of snowballs.

"Okay! Okay!" Wade cried. "If you stop shooting at us, we won't make fun of your smelly feet anymore."

"You better not," Barton snarled, and disappeared behind the pile of snow.

Al-Ian pulled the Tardy Boys and Daisy off the slime ice, and they continued toward The School With No Name. Soon they heard loud shrieking.

"That's strange," said Daisy. "It sounds just like THE SHRIEK OF ULNA MANDIBLE."

"It can't be," said Leyton. "At the end of Book One, she said she was taking Fibby and leaving The School With No Name forever."

But as they got closer, they heard a yell followed by a scream, a shout, a screech, and a shriek.

"That *has* to be Ulna Mandible," Daisy insisted. A moment later, they came around a huge snowdrift and saw Ulna

Mandible's bright red Hummer parked in front of the school. Standing near the school entrance were Principal Stratemeyer and Assistant Principal Snout. Principal Stratemeyer was wearing a long black coat. Assistant Principal Snout was wearing a red ski jacket. He also wore a white breathing mask, bright yellow foam earplugs, and light blue latex gloves.

Principal Stratemeyer and Assistant Principal Snout were listening while Ulna Mandible yelled at them. As usual, Fibby Mandible stood behind her mother while she yelled. Fibby and her mother were dressed in matching tan sheepskin coats.

"I demand that you allow furry animals on school property!" Ulna screamed.

"But I don't understand," said Assistant Principal Snout. "You're the one who wanted the NFA (No Furry Animals) rule."

"That was before my daughter was cured by Dr. Crock!" Ulna Mandible screeched. "Dr. Crock is the world's foremost homeopathic, naturopathic, and psychopathic healer! Thanks to him, my daughter is no longer allergic to fur. And that means she can have the cat she's always wanted!"

"I'm just curious, Mrs. Mandible," said Mr. Stratemeyer. "What medicine did Dr. Crock use to cure Fibby of her allergy?"

"Herbal Sodium Pentothal!" Ulna Mandible shouted.

Al-Ian caught his breath and whispered to his friends, "Sodium Pentothal is truth serum!"

By now Daisy, Al-Ian, and the Tardy

Boys — minus TJ who went to the elementary school — had arrived at the front entrance of the school. Above the entrance hung a big green-and-white banner announcing

CELEBRATE NATIONAL ORAL HYGIENE DAY

When Fibby Mandible saw the Tardy Boys and their friends, she crossed her arms and turned up her nose.

"I thought your mother said she was taking you out of this school forever," Al-Ian said.

"No other school wanted me," Fibby answered. "I mean, we decided to give this school one more chance."

The Tardy Boys and their friends blinked with astonishment. For a moment, Fibby had actually told the truth!

Fibby looked at Daisy's roadkill boots and made a face. "Where did you get those yucky boots?"

"My parents made them out of poor defenseless animals that had been run over by cars," Daisy answered. "Where did you and your mom get your coats?"

"My mom lucked into them at a tag sale," Fibby said. "I mean, they're from Saks Fifth Avenue."

Meanwhile, Ulna screeched, "I insist that you have a Bring Your Pet to School Day so that my daughter can bring her cat to school and show it off."

"When did you get a cat?" Wade asked Fibby.

"I haven't gotten one yet, but I'm going to make my mother buy me one," said Fibby. "Because I love making my mother get me whatever I want."

"If you don't allow furry animals in this school, I'll sue!" Ulna Mandible threatened.

"I will take your request under consideration," said Principal Stratemeyer. "Meanwhile, school has begun, so your daughter should go inside."

Fibby went inside. Her mother got into her red Hummer and drove straight through a huge snowdrift, leaving a big square hole. The Tardy Boys and their friends started to go into school, but Assistant Principal Snout pointed at his watch and said, "Stop! You're late again."

"But so was Fibby," said Leyton.

"No, she wasn't," said Assistant Principal Snout. "She got here half an hour ago and waited while her mother shouted, yelled, screamed, screeched, and shrieked at us. But you four just got here, and that means you're late. What's your excuse this time?"

"We were pinned down by enemy fire," said Leyton.

Assistant Principal Snout frowned.

"Barton Slugg was firing perfectly round snowballs at us with his Super Slammer snowball gun," said Wade.

"And we were trapped on his slime ice and couldn't get away," added Daisy.

"That is the lamest excuse I've ever heard," Assistant Principal Snout said. "Do you really expect me to believe you?"

"You can ask Barton himself," said Daisy pointing across the street. "Here he comes."

Barton was walking toward them with the Super Slammer snowball gun on his shoulder.

"Why are you late?" Assistant Principal Snout asked.

"A little old lady was trying to cross the street, and it was so snowy and icy that I thought I should help her, even though it meant I'd be late," Barton explained.

"That was very nice of you," said Assistant Principal Snout. "Now hurry up and go inside."

"Wait!" Al-Ian said. "What about the Super Slammer snowball gun?"

"Barton, what's that thing on your shoulder?" asked Assistant Principal Snout.

"This?" Barton gestured innocently at the snowball gun. "It's my shoulder-mounted telescope."

"I thought so," said Assistant Principal Snout. "Now go to class." He turned to the

Tardy Boys, Daisy, and Al-Ian. "You four go to my orifice immediately."

"I think you mean *office*," said Daisy.

"Yes," said Assistant Principal Snout. "That, too."

THE SQUEAK TEST

To: Catmander Claw on Planet Hiss in
the Feline Galaxy
From: Cat Spy Scratchy on Planet Earth
in the Milky Way Galaxy

Do not worry about humans. They are
a simpleminded species of two-legged
animals. I do not think they can stop
us from taking over. Humans are easy
to spot because they are the only

creatures left on this planet who
have not yet figured out that they
could run much faster on four legs
than on two.

The Tardy Boys, Daisy, and Al-Ian
wound up in Assistant Principal Snout's
office at least once a day. They spent
more time in that office than anyone in
school except for Assistant Principal
Snout. They spent so much time in
that office that they knew it was an
assistant principal's *office* and not
an assistant principal's *orifice*, which
is a mouthlike opening.

As the Tardy Boys and their friends
walked toward the office, they noticed

that the halls were lined with green-and-white posters. One poster read

DID YOU KNOW THAT
150 MILLION GERMS LIVE IN YOUR MOUTH?

Another said

THE GERMS IN YOUR MOUTH CAN CAUSE
BAD BREATH, CAVITIES, AND GUM DISEASE

By now, they had reached the office. But before they could go in, they had to wash their hands in the sink beside the door. Next, they had to leave their shoes on the mat outside the door. Only then were they allowed to enter.

Inside the office, a large hypoallergenic air purifier hummed. On the shelf behind

Assistant Principal Snout's desk were three large boxes. One contained white breathing masks. Another contained light blue latex gloves. The third contained bright yellow foam earplugs.

Four chairs lined the wall as far from the assistant principal's desk as possible. On the floor between the chairs and the desk was a painted red line. A sign next to the red line said

STUDENTS — DO NOT
CROSS THIS LINE

The Tardy Boys and their friends sat down in the chairs and waited.

"I don't get it," Al-Ian said. "Why does Assistant Principal Snout believe Barton's lies but not believe us when we're telling the truth?"

"He's confuzzled," Leyton said.

The others stared at him. Daisy said, "Leyton, there's no such word."

"Sure there is," Leyton said. "It means he's got everything mixed up."

Daisy and Al-Ian shook their heads.

Leyton crossed his arms stubbornly. "Well, if it isn't a word, it should be."

The office door opened, and Assistant Principal Snout came in. "Did you all brush your teeth, floss, and rinse with mouthwash before coming in here?"

"I thought we just had to wash our hands and take off our shoes," said Daisy.

"Do you know what bacteria are?" asked Assistant Principal Snout.

"They're tiny creepy crawly thingies," said Al-Ian.

"Otherwise known as germs," said Assistant Principal Snout. "And do you have any idea how many of them live in your mouth?"

"One hundred and fifty million," said Wade.

"That's correct," said Assistant Principal Snout, and pointed at the door. "Now all of you, go back out and brush, floss, and rinse."

The Tardy Boys and their friends returned to the sink outside the office. In the medicine cabinet above the sink, they found toothbrushes, toothpaste, floss, and mouthwash.

"I can't believe Assistant Principal Snout is making us do this," Wade said.

"I can't believe there are a hundred and fifty million germs living in my mouth," said Leyton. He opened his mouth and looked in the mirror. "How can they all fit in there?"

"They're microscopic," said Daisy.

"I bet," said Leyton. "And they must be really small, too."

"Have you ever thought about where cheese comes from?" asked Al-Ian while he brushed his teeth.

"Cows," said Leyton. "And sometimes goats. And in Barton Slugg's case, his toes."

"Right, and guess what turns cow's milk and goat's milk and Barton's sock fibers, dead skin cells, and sweat into those cheeses?" asked Al-Ian.

Leyton frowned. "How would I know?"

"Bacteria," said Al-Ian. "In fact, most of the bacteria in our bodies are good bacteria. They assist with digestion and do other helpful stuff."

"Then why does Assistant Principal Snout want us to get rid of them?" asked Leyton.

"Because he's a nut case," said Wade while he flossed.

"Forget it," Leyton said, and dropped his toothbrush in the garbage. "I'm not doing it. I like my bacteria just the way they are."

Leyton waited while the others brushed, flossed, and rinsed. Then they all went back into the office. Assistant Principal Snout was sitting at his desk. He'd removed the bright yellow earplugs. Now that he was safe in his office, he did not have to fear THE SHRIEK OF ULNA MANDIBLE. He'd also taken off his breathing mask. Now that he was in the same room with the hypoallergenic air purifier, he did not have to worry about breathing the same air students breathed. He'd also taken off his blue latex gloves. Now that he was on the other side of the red line, he did not have to worry about touching or being touched by germ-ridden students.

"Stand at attention," Assistant Principal Snout ordered. "Each of you rub your forefinger across your front teeth."

"Why?" asked Leyton.

"It's the squeak test," Al-Ian whispered.

Wade's teeth squeaked when he rubbed them with his finger. So did Daisy's and Al-Ian's. When Leyton rubbed his teeth, they did not squeak.

"Why didn't you clean your teeth?" asked Assistant Principal Snout.

"Because some germs are good," said Leyton.

"Nonsense," said Assistant Principal Snout. "The only good germ is a dead germ. Now go brush, floss, and rinse!"

Leyton went back outside and brushed, flossed, and rinsed. Then he returned to the office and passed the squeak test. The assistant principal stared at the Tardy Boys and their friends for a long time. The lines in his forehead grew deep. "Why are you four sitting there?" he asked.

"You told us to," said Daisy.

Assistant Principal Snout frowned. "Do you remember why?"

Before they could answer, the door to the office swung open and Olga Shotput, the school's silver-medal-winning janitor, rushed in.

"Did you brush, floss, and rinse?" Assistant Principal Snout demanded.

Olga spun around and ran back out of the office. Then she rushed back in.

"I just heard that there's going to be —" she began.

But Assistant Principal Snout cut her short. "Rub your forefinger across your front teeth."

Olga rubbed her finger against her teeth, and they squeaked.

"Good," said Assistant Principal Snout. "You may continue."

"I heard there is going to be a Bring Your Pet to School Day," Olga said.

"Yes, Olga," he said. "That's true."

"But that's terrible!" Olga Shotput cried. "Animals will do their business everywhere! They'll track in dirt and shed fur. I'll lose my silver medal!"

Olga was a large woman with short hair and muscular arms who had come to the United States many years ago to compete

in the Spring Olympics. Her silver medal was the top of a tuna fish can that hung around her neck on a red-white-and-blue ribbon.

"You will not lose your silver medal," said Assistant Principal Snout.

"How do you know?" Olga cried. "Are you on the International Olympic Janitorial Committee?"

"No, but —"

"So you don't know!" Olga cried. "Oh, this is terrible, just terrible! And what about Skating Day? All those skates chipping the paint off lockers! It's awful! I've told you a hundred times, if you want this school to be neat and clean, *don't let students in!*"

Assistant Principal Snout sighed. It was obvious that he would have to take care of Olga and would not be able to yell at the Tardy Boys and their friends. "You four may go," he said. "And if you remember why I wanted you here in the first place, don't do it again."

THE MOTHER OF ALL TOE CHEESE

To: Cat Spy Scratchy on Planet Earth
in the Milky Way Galaxy

From: Catmander Claw on Planet Hiss
in the Feline Galaxy

Are you sure we will be able to
defeat the humans just because they
walk on two legs? Is it possible
that they are more clever than
they appear?

The Tardy Boys had gym three times a week. They were in the locker room changing into their gym clothes when Mr. Circle, the gym teacher, said, "We're going outside."

Loud groans and moans rose all around the locker room.

"How can we go outside, Mr. Circle?" Leyton asked. "It's the dead of winter, and there's six feet of snow on the ground."

"The fresh air will be good for you," Mr. Circle answered.

"That's for sure," Al-Ian muttered. "Anything's better than staying inside with the smell of Barton's toe cheese."

In the next aisle, Barton Slugg heard him. "Mr. Circle!" he shouted.

"What is it, Barton?" Mr. Circle asked.

"Al-Ian is making fun of my feet,"
Barton complained. "It's not fair. It's the
way I was born."

"We were all born with feet, Barton," Mr.
Circle said.

"But they say mine smell," whined
Barton.

"Don't make fun of Barton's feet," Mr.
Circle told Al-Ian.

"Why doesn't he just wash them?"
Al-Ian asked.

"I do," said Barton.

"With soap," said Al-Ian.

"That's enough!" Mr. Circle snapped.
Everyone finished getting into their shorts
and T-shirts and headed outside. As
Barton passed the aisle where the Tardy
Boys and Al-Ian were, he wrinkled his
nose at them. "You guys think you're so

cool," he sneered. "But I get a whole aisle to myself."

This was true. Kids called Barton's aisle the Aisle of Death. Inside Barton's locker was a pair of gym socks that were so old and so dirty that growing in them was THE MOTHER OF ALL TOE CHEESE!

Outside in the snow, the gym class stood around in their shorts and T-shirts shivering while Mr. Circle handed out badminton racquets.

"What should we do with these?" Wade asked through chattering teeth.

"Whatever you like," said Mr. Circle, who went back inside to get warm.

Later that day, after the Tardy Boys and Al-Ian recovered from Gym-induced Frostbite, they went to RePete's Cat Palace to get cat food. RePete's was a large two-story building with a huge, flashing pink neon sign above the door that said CAT PALACE, SPA, AND GROOMING CENTER.

Inside, the brightly lit aisles were filled with everything a cat lover could possibly want.

"Hey, check this out!" Leyton pointed at a rack of CDs in the music section. "Love songs for cats and their owners."

"And here's the cat birthday section," said Al-Ian. "Including birthday cards and party gifts!"

Suddenly, a loud, familiar voice shouted, "I want that one!"

"But it's so expensive!" another familiar voice yelled.

"I don't care!"

"It's Fibby and her mother," Al-Ian whispered, and pointed toward the second floor where a sign said CAT SALES, SPA, AND GROOMING. "They must be up there."

"Let's go see," whispered Leyton.

The Tardy Boys and Al-Ian snuck up the stairs. The second floor was divided into three parts: the Spa, where people left their cats when they went away; the Grooming Center, where people brought their cats to be washed and groomed; and the Sales Center, where the walls were lined with floor-to-ceiling sliding glass windows. Inside the windows were steel cages filled with kittens and cats for sale.

"This is creepy," said Wade as he looked at the cats in the cages.

"It's like, maximum security cat prison," Al-Ian whispered.

Not far away, Fibby and her mother were standing in front of some cages.

"What about that one?" Ulna screeched, pointing at a black-and-white cat.

"I want this one!" Fibby insisted, pointing at a long-haired gray cat.

"But that one's almost five hundred dollars!" Ulna shouted.

"After all this time, I can finally have a cat!" Fibby wailed. "Don't you want me to be happy?"

"I guess Fibby's serious about getting a cat," Leyton whispered.

All the cats in cages weirded Wade out. Nor did he enjoy listening to Fibby and her mom yell at each other. "Let's go back downstairs and look for that special cat food."

On the first floor were aisles filled with cat foods. There were foods for fat cats that wanted to slim down and slim cats that wanted to fatten up. There was food for picky eaters and food for cats that wanted a more luxurious coat. There was food for old cats and young cats, for active cats and inactive cats.

"Wow! Look at this!" Leyton pointed at a huge green bag. "A hundred pounds of cat food. This must be for a really huge cat."

As usual when his brother said something dumb, Wade sighed. "No, Leyton, it's not for a really huge cat. It's probably for someone who has a lot of cats."

"But it could be for one really huge cat," Leyton insisted.

"Believe me, Leyton," Wade said. "No cat is so big that it needs a hundred-pound food bag."

"Oh, yeah, Mr. Smarty-Face?" Leyton crossed his muscular arms and shot back. "What about lions and tigers?"

Wade couldn't believe how thick his brother was. "Lions and tigers eat lion and tiger food, dimwit." Then he turned to Al-Ian. "Which food do you think we should get?"

Al-Ian scratched his head. "I don't know. Maybe we should ask someone."

"Who?" asked Leyton.

"Maybe RePete," said Al-Ian.

"Who?" asked Leyton.

"Re —" Al-Ian started to say.

"Stop!" cried Wade, and pointed to a man sitting beside a cash register behind a glass counter. "We'll ask him."

The man had long gray hair pulled into a ponytail and was wearing a red vest over a yellow turtleneck sweater. On the vest was a name tag that said REPETE.

"How can I help you?" RePete asked.

"We need to find the right food for our cat," said Wade.

"What does your cat like to eat?" asked RePete.

"We don't know," said Leyton.

RePete frowned and the lines in his forehead began to show. "Well, what do you feed him?"

"We don't," said Wade.

RePete's frown grew, and the lines in his forehead deepened.

"Until last week, we didn't even know we had a cat," Leyton said.

The lines in RePete's forehead got so deep that they were probably visible to the catstronomers on Planet Hiss in the Feline Galaxy. Wade explained how they had only just learned that they had a cat and that it was so skinny and sickly that they'd been told they should feed it special cat food.

RePete nodded. "Whoever told you that was absolutely right. A cat that skinny and sickly must be fed very carefully. I know just the food for you. Wait here and I'll be back." He disappeared down the cat food aisle.

The Tardy Boys waited beside the counter. Leyton wondered if there was a Lion and Tiger Palace where people could buy lion and tiger food. Wade wondered if having a name like RePete was more annoying than having a brother who had enough empty space in his skull for monkeys to swing around.

RePete returned with a bag that was the size of a small loaf of bread.

"Nutricat Deluxe?" Leyton read the label.

"This is exactly what your cat needs," RePete said. "That will be twenty dollars, please."

"Seems like a lot for such a small bag of food," said Wade.

RePete stuck his nose in the air. "All right. It's your decision. Pick out whatever cheap cat food you want and feed it to that poor, sick cat. Just don't come crying to me when your little kitty catches the last train to the big litter box in the sky."

"There's a big litter box in the sky?" Leyton asked.

"It's a euphemism," Wade tried to explain. It was a big word he'd learned from the dictionary over the weekend.

"A *who-fuh*-mism?" asked Leyton.

"A you-fuh-mism," Wade repeated.

"A *me-fuh*-mism?" said Leyton.

"I'll explain later," Wade said, and turned back to RePete. "Okay, we'll take it."

Wade paid for the Nutricat Deluxe cat food, and RePete handed him a bright red sheet of paper.

"Perhaps," RePete said, "when your cat is feeling better, you will consider entering him in the Catalent Contest. If your cat wins, you'll get a free one-year supply of Nutricat Deluxe."

"Thanks," Wade said. "We'll definitely think about it."

The Tardy Boys and Al-Ian left RePete's Cat Palace. Outside, the cold air had a sharp, bitter odor that burned the insides of their noses.

"Look!" Leyton pointed down the road. "It's Barton, and he's carrying something!"

"It must be the Super Slammer!" Al-Ian gasped.

FLUFFERNUTTER-IN-A-JAR

To: Catmander Claw on Planet Hiss in
the Feline Galaxy

From: Cat Spy Scratchy on Planet Earth
in the Milky Way Galaxy

Sir, I am confident that we will have
no problem defeating the humans.
Cats on this planet have already
trained humans to house them, feed

them, pet them, and scratch them
behind the ears.

The Tardy Boys and Al-Ian dove into the closest snowbank. The heavy, wet snow felt icy against their faces and hands and made them shiver as it seeped in around their collars while they hid, waiting for Barton to pass.

But Barton didn't pass. He stopped beside the snowbank. "What's wrong with you morons?" he asked. "Did you really think I didn't see you?"

Wade and the others stuck their heads out of the snow. Now that Barton was close, the odor of his toe cheese was strong. But they could see that he wasn't

carrying the Super Slammer snowball
gun. He was carrying a cat carrier.

The Tardy Boys and Al-Ian crawled out
of the snowbank and brushed the snow
off their clothes. "What's in the cat
carrier?" asked Leyton.

"My goldfish," answered Barton.

"Really?" said Leyton.

"No, you numbskull," Barton snapped.
"It's my cat, Tinker Bell. Today's her
weekly grooming appointment."

"Why do you have your cat groomed
every week?" Al-Ian asked.

"Because Tinker Bell is a rare, exotic
shaded silver Persian show cat," Barton
said. "We enter her in cat shows." His
beady eyes focused on the bag of Nutricat
Deluxe cat food in Wade's hands. "What
kind of cat do you have?"

Wade and Leyton shared a nervous

look. They had no idea what kind of cat Skinny was.

"Uh, he's a rare exotic gray-and-white skinny scruffy," Leyton finally said.

"That's a good one," Barton snorted. "There's no such breed as a skinny scruffy."

"It's brand-new," Leyton said. "A scruffy is a mixture of a scrappy and a fluffy."

"Then it's a mixed breed!" Barton said with a laugh.

"So?" said Leyton.

"If you knew anything about cats, you'd know that mixed breeds are the lowest of the low," said Barton. "They're not even allowed near a cat show. You guys are so pathetic!" Snickering to himself, Barton headed toward RePete's Cat Palace.

Later, when the Tardy Boys got home, TJ was sitting in the den, watching TV.

"Did you get the special cat food?" he asked.

"Yes," answered Wade. "Where's Skinny Kitty?"

"In the kitchen, I think," said TJ. "I'm really hungry. Did you get anything for dinner?"

Wade realized that he'd spent all his money on the Nutricat Deluxe cat food. "Sorry, little dude. Looks like it's Fluffernutter sandwiches again."

A few weeks earlier, there'd been a big sale on Fluffernutter-in-a-jar at the local food store, and Wade had bought a lifetime supply. Since then, they'd eaten Fluffernutter sandwiches for breakfast, lunch, and dinner, and they were sick of the stuff.

"There's no bread for sandwiches," said TJ. "Can't we order in?"

"Sorry," Wade answered as he and Leyton went into the kitchen. The tattered backpack lay on the kitchen table. Leyton opened it. Inside was Skinny Kitty.

"I don't think he's moved all day," said Leyton.

"You sure he's still alive?" Wade asked.

Leyton reached in and took out Skinny Kitty. "He feels warm and he's breathing."

"Go ahead and feed him," Wade said.

Leyton hated it when his brother bossed him around. "Why can't you feed him?" he asked.

"Because I have to study vocabulary so someday I can win a scholarship to college," Wade said.

"What about me?" Leyton asked. "Don't I have to win a scholarship, too?"

Wade knew there was no way his

brother could win a scholarship, unless it was for having a brain with enough empty space inside to fit a Mack truck.

"I know what you're thinking!" Leyton said angrily. "You think I'll never win a scholarship because I didn't know what a *yoo-fuh-fism* was."

"It's euphemism," Wade explained. "And it's pronounced like this: yoo-feh-mizim."

"Whatever!" Leyton shrugged angrily.

"Just feed the cat," Wade said, and headed toward his room.

"You think you're so smart!" Leyton yelled after him. "But if you were really smart, you wouldn't be learning *someone else*'s vocabulary. You'd invent your own!" Wade didn't answer, so Leyton opened the bag of Nutricat Deluxe and poured some in a bowl for Skinny Kitty. It was dinnertime and Leyton was hungry, so he looked in the kitchen cabinets and refrigerator, but all he found was mustard, soy sauce, and thirty-two containers of Fluffernutter-in-a-jar.

Leyton sat down at the kitchen table again. He knew he wasn't as dumb as Wade thought. There might have been room in his skull for monkeys to swing on branches, eat bananas, and pick fleas off one another's backs. But after humans, monkeys were the next smartest animals, except maybe for dolphins. Not only that, but Leyton knew what plenty of words meant. He bet he knew what every word on the label on the cat food bag meant. It said that Nutricat Deluxe was made with "fresh, human-quality ingredients such as a delectable blend of premium all-natural chicken, liver, and turkey, along with fresh vegetables and grasses that appealed to even the most discriminating palate."

Leyton looked down at Skinny Kitty, who'd managed to eat about half the food in his bowl and was now lying on the floor, asleep. Meanwhile, Leyton's own stomach rumbled loudly and hungrily. He wasn't exactly sure what a discriminating palate was, but that delectable blend of premium all-natural chicken, liver, and turkey sounded a lot better than another meal of Fluffernutter-in-a-jar.

Leyton glanced at the doorway. TJ was in the den watching TV and Wade was probably upstairs in his room, learning more big, dumb words. Leyton quietly got another bowl out of the kitchen cabinet. He mixed together some mustard and soy sauce and Nutricat Deluxe. Then he dipped a spoon in and sniffed it.

It smelled mostly like soy sauce and mustard.

He opened his mouth and nibbled a little.

It didn't taste so bad.

In fact, it tasted pretty darn good!

DOODLEY-SQUAT

To: Cat Spy Scratchy on Planet Earth
   in the Milky Way Galaxy

From: Catmander Claw on Planet Hiss
   in the Feline Galaxy

We are still concerned that humans
may be more intelligent than you
think. Please provide more proof
that they are really so simpleminded.

Wade studied vocabulary until his brain hurt. By then he was also really hungry, so he went down to the kitchen. Leyton was watching cartoons on the TV at the kitchen counter.

"You're not going to win a scholarship by watching TV," Wade said.

"Oh, yeah?" said Leyton. "I bet you don't know what the word *gigglesnort* means."

"That's because there's no such word," said Wade.

"There is now," said Leyton. "You know how some cartoon characters snort when they giggle? That's a gigglesnort."

"Great," Wade muttered. "So, did Skinny Kitty eat much?"

"Uh, yeah, he ate a ton," said Leyton.

Wade looked down at the little cat sleeping on the floor. Then he looked in the bag of Nutricat Deluxe. The bag was almost empty! Wade could hardly believe it! "Wow, Skinny Kitty really must have been hungry."

Leyton burped. "Yeah."

Wade looked again at Skinny Kitty. The little cat didn't look big enough to have eaten all that food. Still, there was no other explanation. "Well, that's great. If Skinny Kitty keeps eating like this, he'll get better in no time. I just wish we had something besides Fluffernutter-in-a-jar to eat. Aren't you sick of it?"

"It's not so bad," said Leyton.

"We need to get some other food tomorrow," Wade said. "Only it looks like we're gonna have to get more Nutricat

Deluxe, too, and I don't think we can afford both." Then he had a thought. "Remember the talent contest RePete told us about?"

"RePete?" TJ said as he entered the kitchen.

"Remember the talent —" Wade began to say, then caught himself. "What am I doing?" He shook his head wearily and went out to the hall to get the bright red sheet of paper. "If we can win this contest, we'll get a year's supply of Nutricat Deluxe and we won't go broke paying for cat food."

"Sounds like a good idea," said Leyton, rubbing his full belly.

"But to win the contest Skinny Kitty has to have a talent," said TJ. "I saw this show on TV once where animals did amazing tricks. They had this one cat that could shred an entire roll of toilet paper in thirty seconds."

"Leyton, go get a roll of toilet paper," Wade said.

"Why don't you go?" Leyton snapped back. Not only did he hate it when his brother bossed him around, but his stomach was full and he didn't feel like moving.

Wade glared at his brother and then got a roll of toilet paper. He put it on the floor. Skinny Kitty looked at the roll of toilet paper, then yawned, rolled over, and went back to sleep.

"There was a cat that could jump up and turn a doorknob and open a door," said TJ. "And another that could flush a toilet. And one that could walk on its hind legs. And . . ."

TJ recited the list of things that he'd seen talented cats do on TV. Wade tried to get Skinny Kitty to do them, but all Skinny Kitty wanted to do was lie on the floor and sleep.

"Give up, Wade," Leyton finally said. "This cat can't do doodley-squat."

Meowrrrooooowwwwwwlllll!!!! Suddenly, Skinny Kitty screamed and jumped to his feet, coughing, gasping, and choking. He sounded like he was doing to die!

HAIR BALL

To: Catmander Claw on Planet Hiss in
the Feline Galaxy

From: Cat Spy Scratchy on Planet Earth
in the Milky Way Galaxy

Sir, here is proof of how
simpleminded humans are. Dogs on this
planet have invented long strips of
nylon so that they can lead humans
around when they go outside. They

have even trained humans to carry
plastic bags in order to pick up
after them. Can you imagine?

The Tardy Boys watched in fear as
Skinny Kitty coughed and choked.

"What's wrong with him?" TJ cried.

"I don't have a clue," said Wade.

"It's like he's choking on something,"
said Leyton.

"You may have to do CPR, Leyton,"
said Wade.

"I don't know how to do cat CPR," said
Leyton.

Skinny Kitty kept making awful gagging
sounds.

"He's gonna die if we don't do
something!" TJ cried.

Wade ran to the phone and dialed Daisy's number.

"Peace and love," Daisy's hippie mother, Mrs. Peduncle, answered the phone.

"Hi, is Daisy there?" Wade asked.

"Yes, but she's meditating," her mom said.

"I know that's probably pretty important, but we've got a life-and-death cat emergency here and we need her help," Wade said.

"If your cat dies, I can make it into a hat," said Mrs. Peduncle.

"Uh . . . yeah, sure, thanks," said Wade. "So, can I speak to Daisy?"

"Just a minute," Mrs. Peduncle said. Wade waited anxiously. He could hear loud cat coughing and gagging coming from the kitchen.

"Hello?" Daisy said.

"Daisy, it's Wade. Skinny Kitty's choking to death!" Just then, Skinny Kitty let out a particularly loud, rasping cry.

"Oh, my gosh!" Daisy gasped on the phone. "I heard that! I'll come right over!"

Wade hung up and made a beeline back to the feline. Skinny Kitty was still writhing and gagging on the floor.

"What's he doing?" TJ wondered.

"He could be snarfing," said Leyton.

Wade stared at his brother for a moment. "Okay, what's *snarfing* mean?"

Leyton pretended to be surprised. "*You* don't know, Mr. Smarty-Face?"

"How could I possibly know?" Wade asked. "You just made up the word."

"Snarfing is what happens when you laugh so hard that whatever you just drank comes out your nose," Leyton said.

"Skinny Kitty hasn't had anything to eat

or drink in at least two hours," Wade pointed out. "And nothing's coming out of his nose."

"Then it could be a delayed snarf," said Leyton.

The doorbell rang and TJ ran to answer it.

Bluuuuurrrrpppp! Just then Skinny Kitty made the loudest, most disgusting barfing sound yet. Wade and Leyton jumped back just as Skinny Kitty coughed something gray and slimy onto the floor.

"What is *that*?!" Leyton gasped.

"Oh, thank goodness!" Daisy cried as she hurried into the room.

"Thank goodness for what?" Leyton asked.

Daisy pointed at the slimy gray thing on the floor. "Thank goodness for that."

"What's good about that?" asked Wade.

"It's a hair ball," Daisy explained. "Cats cough them up all the time. Skinny Kitty's going to be fine."

"It's gross," said TJ.

"Not really," said Daisy. "Cats clean their fur by licking themselves. And some of the fur gets swallowed. When a lot of fur collects in a cat's stomach, it becomes a hair ball and the cat has to cough it up."

"Then you know what would happen if a cat swallowed a ball of yarn?" TJ asked.

"What?" Daisy asked with a frown.

"Instead of kittens, it would have mittens!" said TJ.

Daisy noticed the bag of Nutricat Deluxe on the kitchen table. "Oh, I'm so glad you

got the special cat food! Did Skinny Kitty eat it?"

"Tons." Wade held up the bag and shook it to demonstrate that it was nearly empty.

"Amazing!" Daisy said, staring down at Skinny Kitty, who was licking his paw. "He doesn't look big enough to have eaten all that."

"You never know," Leyton said, and burped again. The burp tasted of mustard, soy sauce, and Nutricat Deluxe.

"It's kind of a problem for us," Wade said. "This bag cost twenty bucks. It would really help if Skinny Kitty had a talent." He explained how they could win a year's worth of Nutricat Deluxe if Skinny Kitty won the upcoming talent contest at RePete's Cat Palace.

"What talents do cats have?" Daisy asked.

"That's what we're trying to figure out," said Wade. "And so far, no luck."

Leyton stood up. He burped again, patted his stomach, and yawned. "Maybe we should sleep on it."

BAD
BREATH
IN
STUDENTS

To: Cat Spy Scratchy on Planet Earth
in the Milky Way Galaxy
From: Catmander Claw on Planet Hiss
in the Feline Galaxy

This is very good news. If dogs lead
humans around by leashes, then humans
must indeed be simpleminded and easy

to conquer. Please set up a base of
operations and use direct-hypnotic
staring to take control of as many
cats and humans as possible.

The next day in school, the Tardy Boys
and Daisy walked down the hall toward
Ms. Fitt's social studies class. They were
discussing the Catalent Contest when,
suddenly, a sharp, bitter odor began to
burn their noses. Ahead, a trail of
glimmering slime crossed their path
in the hallway. They turned the corner
and there was the one, the only, Barton
Slugg.

"I heard you talking about the Catalent
Contest," he said with a snarl that

revealed his buckteeth. "Don't tell me you're thinking of entering your crummy mixed-breed cat in it."

"Why not?" asked Leyton.

"What talent does it have?"

"What talent does *your* cat have?" Daisy shot back.

"Tinker Bell's talent is her beauty," Barton said.

"Beauty isn't a talent," Daisy said. "It's something you're born with."

"No way," Barton argued. "It takes work and talent to be as beautiful as Tinker Bell. You think just any old cat can be as beautiful as mine?"

By now, they'd reached Ms. Fitt's class. Ms. Fitt had red hair that hung down past her shoulders in ringlets. She liked to wear big earrings and colorful clothes. Today she was wearing a bright yellow turtleneck sweater, an orange felt skirt, and red-and-blue cowboy boots. Ms. Fitt was everybody's favorite teacher because she liked kids and made learning fun.

"Come on, come on," she waved at them. "Everyone into your seats. We have a very interesting day today."

But before she could close the door, Assistant Principal Snout stepped into the room, followed by a short man wearing a white medical jacket. The man had a long gray beard, wore thick glasses, and had dark tufts of hair growing out of both ears.

"Students, I've brought a special guest to school this afternoon," said the assistant principal. "His name is Dr. Ican Yankum and he's a dentist. He's visiting each class to explain the importance of oral hygiene."

Fibby Mandible raised her hand. "Excuse

me, but my mother would be very upset if she knew that you were interrupting social studies to deal with non-social-studies-related issues."

Had any other student spoken to him like that, Assistant Principal Snout would have given them a month of detention. But Fibby's mother was Ulna Mandible, who loved to come to school and shriek at him. And nothing — not even a mouth filled with 150 million germs — scared Assistant Principal Snout more than THE SHRIEK OF ULNA MANDIBLE.

"Well, Fibby, social studies is the study of being social," he said. "And in order to be social, it helps to have good oral hygiene. After all, no one likes to talk to people with bad breath, yucky teeth, and mouths filled with millions of germs."

Then Assistant Principal Snout left the room, and Dr. Yankum told them about the importance of daily brushing, flossing, and rinsing with mouthwash. When he was finished, he invited kids to ask questions.

"My mother makes me floss and it's a real pain," one kid said. "Is it really necessary?"

"Absolutely," Dr. Yankum answered. "Flossing is very important for maintaining the health of your gums. It also helps get rid of bad breath by removing food trapped between your teeth."

Most of the kids in the class looked completely bored, but Wade noticed that Barton was taking careful notes on everything Dr. Yankum said. Then Barton raised his hand. "What if it's not your mouth that smells, but your feet?"

"Hmm." Dr. Yankum rubbed his chin. "Let me think about that."

When there were no more questions, Dr. Yankum left.

"Well, that certainly was an excellent use of a class period," Ms. Fitt grumbled (Wade suspected she was being sarcastic). "We only have ten minutes left. Does anyone have anything they want to talk about?"

Leyton raised his hand. "Do you think beauty is a talent?"

Ms. Fitt frowned. "That's a strange question. Why do you ask?"

Leyton explained about the Catalent Contest.

"I'm going to enter my cat in that

contest," Fibby said. "Because I have to win everything."

"Since when do you have a cat?" Barton asked her.

"Since yesterday, when I made my mother buy me one," said Fibby.

"What talent does it have?" Barton asked.

"I don't know yet because I only got him yesterday," said Fibby. "But if he doesn't have a talent, I'm going to make my mother go back to the Cat Palace and buy me a more expensive cat that does. And if the Cat Palace doesn't have one, I'll make her go to Just for Cats, and if they don't have one, I'll make her search the whole world until she finds the most talented cat there is so I can win the contest."

"No way," said Barton. "Tinker Bell is

going to win because beauty is a talent and Tinker Bell is the most beautiful cat in the world."

"Wait a minute, what about my brother's question?" said Wade to Ms. Fitt. "Is beauty a talent?"

"I think some people have to work very hard to be beautiful," said Ms. Fitt. "And to a lucky few, beauty just comes naturally. I'd like to enter my cat in that contest. I named him Anestofleas, after the Greek god of tiny, itchy insects."

"I named my cat after Peter Pan's little fairy friend, Tinker Bell," said Barton.

"My cat's name is Purrfect," said Fibby. "I named him after myself."

"You're not perfect," said Barton.

"No, I'm Fibby," said Fibby.

The bell rang. Out in the hall, Barton gloated at the Tardy Boys. "You guys and your scruffy mixed-breed cat are so going to lose!"

"That's what you think," Wade replied. "We have to go back to the Cat Palace today to get more cat food and, while we're there, we'll ask RePete if *he* thinks beauty is a talent."

"Well, I'm going, too," said Barton. "I left Tinker Bell for an overnight grooming and I have to go get her. So we can all hear what RePete has to say."

SNIRT

To: Catmander Claw on Planet Hiss in
the Feline Galaxy
From: Cat Spy Scratchy on Planet Earth
in the Milky Way Galaxy

I have set up a base of operations
at RePete's Cat Palace, which is a
place where cats send their humans to
get the finest food, catnip, toys,

and other important supplies. I will
begin taking over the minds of cats
and humans right away.

After school, they all went to RePete's
Cat Palace. Barton walked ahead of them,
leaving a trail of slippery, smelly slime
ice. The Tardy Boys and their friends kept
falling.

"Do you have to walk in front of us?"
Al-Ian asked.

"Or at least walk faster," said Leyton.
"So we don't have to be so close to
your feet."

"I'm so tired of you guys making fun of
my feet," Barton muttered.

"Then why don't you do something
about them?" Daisy asked.

"Maybe I will," Barton said, and crossed to the other side of the street.

"He's such a slork," Leyton whispered once Barton was out of earshot.

"What's a slork?" Wade asked.

"A slow dork," Leyton explained.

"What if he was a fast dork?" asked Daisy.

"Then he'd be a fork," said Leyton.

A few minutes later, they got to the Cat Palace. "This is amazing," Daisy said. "A whole store just for cats?"

"No," said Leyton. "Just for Cats is on the other side of town. This is the Cat Palace."

"Yes, but what she means is, this store is just for cats," said Wade.

"No," said Leyton. "I just told you. Just for Cats is on the other side of town."

Wade sighed. There was no use trying to explain what he meant.

Inside the Cat Palace, RePete was too busy helping customers to talk about whether beauty was a talent.

"I want to see what's upstairs," said Daisy, climbing the steps. Wade and Al-Ian followed. At the top of the stairs, Daisy suddenly stopped and pointed at the rows of cats and kittens in cages behind the glass windows. "This is terrible! These cats should be in homes, not in cages. I'm going. It's too mean here."

With red, tear-streaked eyes, Daisy hurried back down the stairs.

"Gee," said Al-Ian to Wade as they followed, "the last time she got this upset was when we had to dissect worms in science class."

By now, Leyton had gotten a new bag of Nutricat Deluxe, and Barton had picked up Tinker Bell. Barton's cat was indeed beautiful. She had long, thick, soft gray fur and amazing blue eyes. If RePete decided that beauty was a talent, there was no doubt in anyone's mind that Tinker Bell would win.

Only a few customers were still around the counter and, as soon as Barton joined them, they began to pinch their noses and wave their hands in front of their faces.

"What's that awful smell?" asked a woman.

"I don't know, but I'm getting out of here," said someone else.

People began fleeing the store. On the other side of the counter, RePete watched with a puzzled look. "Where's everyone going?" he asked. "And what's that terrible smell?"

"It's nothing," said Barton. "Just some random smell that comes and goes."

"I hope it goes soon," said RePete. "Or I'll go out of business."

Al-Ian noticed that on a shelf behind RePete, an orange-striped cat lay on a plush purple pillow. It had the yellowest eyes he'd ever seen and, when it looked at him, Al-Ian felt all tingly and strange.

"Excuse me, RePete?" Leyton said.

RePete looked up. "I didn't say anything."

"Er, uh, right," said Leyton. "Anyway, we have a question. Will beauty count as a talent in the Catalent Contest?"

RePete rubbed his chin thoughtfully. At the same moment, the orange-striped cat

on the purple pillow saw Barton take
Tinker Bell out of the cat carrier. The
orange-striped cat widened its bright
yellow eyes and stared at Tinker Bell.

RePete started to shake his head. "I don't
see why beauty should count as a —"

The orange-striped cat turned its head
and stared at RePete. It made a soft
hissing sound, and its bright yellow eyes
began to glow. RePete stood behind the
counter without moving or speaking.

"RePete?" Wade said.

"Huh?" RePete seemed to wake as if
from a daze.

"You started to say that you didn't see
why beauty should count as a . . . and
then you stopped," Wade said. "What
were you going to say?"

RePete glanced at the orange-striped
cat, then back at the boys. His eyes had a

glassy look. "I was going to say that I don't see why beauty . . . shouldn't count as a talent."

"Wait," said Al-Ian. "That's not what you were going to say."

"Yes, it was," said RePete.

"Aha!" Barton cried. "He thinks beauty is a talent! And since there's no cat in the world more beautiful than Tinker Bell, she's going to win!"

Al-Ian didn't know if he was imagining things, but it almost looked like the orange-striped cat smiled.

"Unless another cat comes up with a talent that's even greater than beauty," Leyton said.

"Yeah, right." Barton scoffed and placed Tinker Bell back in her carrier. "See you at the Catalent Contest. Be prepared to lose."

Wade paid for the bag of Nutricat

Deluxe. Then he, Leyton, and Al-Ian left RePete's Cat Palace.

"Did you guys notice that orange-striped cat behind the counter?" Al-Ian asked as they walked home. "The one with the yellow eyes?"

"I did," said Wade. "What about it?"

"Didn't you think it was weird?" Al-Ian asked.

"No," said Wade.

Al-Ian turned to Leyton, who was staring down at the dirty gray snow that had been plowed up along the side of the road.

"What about you, Leyton?" said Al-Ian. "Did you notice anything strange?"

"Snirt," said Leyton.

"What?" said Al-Ian.

"It's snirt," said Leyton. "This dirty gray

snow. It's a combination of snow and dirt . . . snirt."

"Let me guess," groaned Wade. "This is another one of your new words?"

"It makes sense, doesn't it?" Leyton asked.

"No, it doesn't," Wade snapped. "People don't go around combining old words to make new ones. If they did, you'd have all kinds of dumb words. I mean, what would stop someone from combining words like smoke and fog? Or cafeteria and auditorium? Or spoon and fork?"

"Wait," said Al-Ian. "I was talking about the orange-striped cat. Didn't you guys notice anything strange about what just happened with RePete?"

"Are you joking?" Wade asked. "The *whole thing* seemed strange to me. I still don't understand why beauty should be a talent."

"Sure, but did *anything else* seem strange to you?" asked Al-Ian.

"Like what?" asked Wade.

"Remember how we asked RePete if beauty was a talent?" Al-Ian said. "It looked like he was going to say no."

"And then he said yes," said Wade.

"Exactly!" said Al-Ian. "And did you see why he changed his mind?"

Wade and Leyton shared a puzzled look. "Of course not," said Wade. "We can't see why someone changes their mind. It happens inside their head."

"So you didn't see what the orange-striped cat did?" Al-Ian asked.

Leyton and Wade shook their heads.

"It stared at RePete and its eyes glowed,"

said Al-Ian. "It was *controlling* RePete's thoughts!"

"Oh, right!" Leyton chuckled. "Let me guess. It's the Cat from Another Planet!"

"I'm serious!" Al-Ian said.

"You're always serious when it comes to aliens," Leyton said. "You think they're everywhere! They're driving cars. They're hiding behind snowbanks. They're watching us from rooftops." He suddenly pointed into the sky. "Look! There goes one now!"

"How can you joke about aliens when your own parents were kidnapped by them?" Al-Ian asked.

"That's different," Leyton said. "Those aliens must have come from some faraway planet. But you think aliens are everywhere."

Al-Ian shook his head and sighed wearily. It was no use trying to convince them. They'd gotten to his street, and it was time to go. "I'll see you guys tomorrow."

"If you haven't been kidnapped by aliens," Leyton teased. He and Wade continued toward home. Ahead was the grocery store.

"Now that we've paid for the Nutricat Deluxe," Wade said, "we have two dollars left. I guess we better see what we can get."

A few minutes later, they left the grocery store with a loaf of bread.

"I can't believe we're having Fluffernutter sandwiches again for dinner," Wade moaned.

"It won't be so bad," said Leyton, holding the bag of Nutricat Deluxe close.

SKINNY KITTY HAS A TALENT!

To: Cat Spy Scratchy on Planet Earth
in the Milky Way Galaxy

From: His Royal Majesty King Kat on
Planet Hiss in the Feline Galaxy

Catmander Claw has told me about your
discovery of the dim-witted humans
on Planet Earth. He said that cats
and dogs have trained them. It sounds
like it will be very easy to take

over their minds and enslave them.
Good work. When you return to our
planet, you will be given a hero's
welcome and a fresh piece of fish.

At home, Wade, Leyton, and TJ sat at the kitchen table and stared at their Fluffernutter sandwiches.

"Couldn't you buy something else for dinner?" TJ groaned.

"Sorry, little dude, but the rest of the money went toward food for Skinny Kitty," Wade said.

"We better win the Catalent Contest," said TJ.

He and Wade forced themselves to eat their Fluffernutter sandwiches. Leyton didn't touch his.

"Aren't you going to eat?" Wade asked him.

"Sooner or later," Leyton said.

"Why don't you feed Skinny Kitty and see if he has any talents while I study vocabulary," Wade said, getting up.

Instead of arguing, Leyton said, "Okay."

Leyton waited until TJ and Wade left the kitchen and then made two bowls of Nutricat Deluxe—one with mustard and soy sauce for himself and one for Skinny Kitty. After the skinny, scruffy cat finished eating, he rubbed himself against Leyton's leg and purred. Leyton was surprised. This was the first time Skinny Kitty had moved for anything except food. The cat looked up at Leyton, and its green eyes twinkled for a moment. Then he stretched and lay down on the floor to sleep.

After a while, Wade returned to the kitchen and picked up the new bag of Nutricat Deluxe. "I don't believe it! It's almost empty! How can that little cat eat so much?"

Leyton burped and tasted soy sauce, mustard, and Nutricat Deluxe. "Must be making up for lost time."

Wade shook his head in disbelief. "TJ was right. If Skinny Kitty doesn't win the Catalent Contest, we're not going to have enough food to feed all of us. Did you find out if he has any talents?"

Leyton shook his head. "Forget it, Wade. This cat can't do doodley-squat."

No sooner did the words leave his mouth than Skinny Kitty screamed *Meowrrrooooowwwwwwwllllll!!!!* and started to writhe and gag and cough!

"Oh, no, not again!" Leyton gasped.

"It's gonna be okay," Wade said. "Remember what Daisy said? Cats do this all the time."

"Maybe, but it's still freaky," Leyton said.

"You want to know what's really freaky?" Wade said, then moved close and whispered into his brother's ear. "Each time you say doodley-squat, Skinny Kitty starts to cough up a hair ball."

"Doodley-squat?" Leyton repeated loudly.

Meowrrrooooowwwwwwwllllll!!!! Skinny Kitty screamed and twisted as he kept choking.

"Keep it down!" Wade hissed at Leyton. "You're torturing him." Wade grabbed his brother's sleeve and pulled him out of the kitchen. "Not only do we have a cat that's eating up all our money and doesn't have any talents, but now we have to watch what we say around it."

"Bummer," Leyton agreed, although he really didn't care as long as there was enough Nutricat Deluxe in the house for another meal.

"Wait a minute!" Wade suddenly cried. "That means Skinny Kitty *does* have a talent. Every time you say doodley-squat, he coughs up a hair ball!"

"That's not a talent," Leyton said.

"What would you call it?" Wade asked.

"Urp!" Before Leyton could answer, he burped.

Wade took a sniff and made a face. "That's weird. It smells like mustard, soy sauce, and cat food." Then he gave his brother a strange look.

ALIEN SPACE CAT MIND CONTROL

To: Cat Spy Scratchy on Planet Earth in
the Milky Way Galaxy

From: Catmander Claw on Planet Hiss in
the Feline Galaxy

Several days have passed since your
last communication, Cat Spy Scratchy.
Is everything okay? Are you still
taking over as many human and cat
minds as possible? We have begun

preparations for the Hisstorian
attack of Planet Earth.

Bring Your Pet to School Day was scheduled for Saturday morning from ten until noon. Carrying Skinny Kitty in the old tattered backpack, Wade and Leyton walked to school. It was a very cold day, and they were bundled up in puffy jackets, hats, and gloves.

Outside The School With No Name, they ran into Daisy and Al-Ian. Al-Ian was also dressed in a puffy jacket, hat, and gloves, while Daisy wore her long coat and roadkill boots. She was holding Wheezy in her arms. The little, old pug dog was dressed in a light blue sweater. Matching booties covered his paws and a little blue knit cap rested on his head. Al-Ian was carrying a small clear plastic cage. Inside was blue gravel, a plastic miniature brown-and-green palm tree, and a round shell.

"I didn't know you had a pet," said Leyton.

"Yes, this is Kermit the hermit crab," said Al-Ian.

"Does Kermit have a talent?" Daisy asked.

"Now and then one of his legs falls off," said Al-Ian.

Cars were pulling into the parking lot, and kids were getting out with their pets. RePete got out of a gray sedan and walked toward them carrying a blue cat carrier.

"I wonder why he's coming to Bring Your Pet to School Day," said Al-Ian.

Assistant Principal Snout came out. As usual, he was wearing a white face mask, yellow earplugs, and blue latex gloves. "Late again!" he grumbled, and gestured at his wristwatch. "It's after ten A.M., and school started at eight."

"But it's Saturday," said Wade.

Assistant Principal Snout blinked. "It is?"

"Do you ever go home?" Daisy asked.

Assistant Principal Snout hung his head sadly. "It's lonely there."

"You stay here at school all the time?" Leyton asked.

"Most of the time," Assistant Principal Snout answered. "Sometimes I leave to eat or run errands."

By now, RePete had joined them. In the blue cat carrier was the orange-striped cat.

"May I help you?" said Assistant Principal Snout.

"I am here for Bring Your Pet to School Day," said RePete.

"I'm sorry," Assistant Principal Snout started to say. "But Bring Your Pet to School Day is only for —" His voice trailed off as he stared at the orange-striped cat in the cat carrier. The cat hissed softly, and its bright yellow eyes glowed. Assistant Principal Snout stood in front of the school entrance without moving or speaking.

"Hello?" Al-Ian said.

"Huh?" Assistant Principal Snout seemed to wake from a daze.

"You started to say that Bring Your Pet to School Day is only for . . . and then you stopped," Wade said.

"Uh, right," said Assistant Principal Snout. His eyes looked glassy.

"What were you going to say?" asked Wade.

Assistant Principal Snout glanced at the

orange-striped cat in the cat carrier. "I was going to say that Bring Your Pet to School Day is only for students and Cat Palace owners with long gray ponytails." He held the school door open. "Please go right in."

Inside school, Al-Ian pulled his friends aside and whispered, "Did you see that!? Assistant Principal Snout was going to say that Bring Your Pet to School Day was only for students. And then that orange-striped cat stared at him, and he added that it was for students *and* Cat Palace owners with long gray ponytails."

The Tardy Boys and Daisy glanced at one another uncertainly.

"So?" Wade said.

"That cat took control of Assistant Principal Snout's mind," Al-Ian said.

Wade, Leyton, and Daisy grinned.

"I'm serious!" Al-Ian insisted. "It's the same exact thing that happened to RePete at the Cat Palace when we asked him if beauty was a talent. He was going to say no and then changed his answer to yes. When that orange-striped cat stares at you with those glowing yellow eyes, it takes control of your mind."

"Cat mind control?" Wade asked with a smile.

"Not just cat mind control," Al-Ian said. "Alien Space Cat Mind Control! I'm serious! Have you ever seen a cat that had eyes that glowed?"

"Did you see its eyes glow?" Daisy asked Wade.

Wade shook his head.

"That cat is not from this planet," Al-Ian insisted. "There's only one place in the whole universe where they teach mind control, and that's on Planet Hocus in the Pocus Galaxy."

By now, Daisy and the Tardy Boys had very wide smiles.

"Okay, don't believe me," Al-Ian snapped angrily. "But I'm warning you. Whatever you do, don't look straight into that cat's eyes."

The Tardy Boys and their friends went into the gym. Tables were set up in long rows lined with cages, aquariums, and animal carriers. Wade and Leyton took Skinny Kitty out of the tattered backpack and placed him on a table. A large crowd had gathered around the table next to theirs. The people in the crowd were ooohing and ahhing.

"I've never seen such a beautiful cat," one person said.

"Absolutely gorgeous," said another.

Wade stretched up on his toes and looked over the crowd.

"Whose cat is it?" Daisy asked.

"Barton's," Wade said.

"And look who's right next to it!" said Al-Ian.

On the table beside Tinker Bell was the orange-striped cat, staring at Tinker Bell as if it couldn't tear its yellow eyes away.

Barton came through the crowd. He'd combed his messy brown hair off his forehead. "Notice anything different?"

"You combed your hair?" guessed Daisy.

"Not that," said Barton.

"Five out of four people have trouble with fractions?" guessed Leyton.

"Not that," said Barton.

"Then what?" asked Wade.

"My feet," Barton said.

Something *was* different. The awful,

bitter stench of Barton's unwashed feet was gone! Each of Barton's shoes was inside a thick, clear plastic bag!

"No more smell," Barton said. "As long as my feet are encased in these smell-resistant bags, they're just like everyone else's feet."

"But you can't go through life with your feet in bags," Daisy said.

"Why not?" asked Barton.

Before Wade and the others could respond, they were jostled by the crowd growing around Tinker Bell's table.

"See?" Barton said. "Everybody loves Tinker Bell."

"That doesn't mean she has a talent," Wade said.

"Oh, yeah?" Barton pointed at the table where the Tardy Boys had left Skinny Kitty. Wade was surprised to see that

Skinny Kitty was on his feet, staring at the orange-striped cat. And the orange-striped cat was staring at Skinny Kitty. Its back was arched and its claws and teeth were bared. Its yellow eyes glowed, and it let out a long, harsh hiss.

"Tinker Bell's got more talent than that sorry-looking bag of bones," said Barton.

"You might be surprised," said Leyton.

Barton's forehead wrinkled and his eyebrows dipped.

Meanwhile, the orange-striped cat hissed at Skinny Kitty again. Wade wondered why, out of all the cats in the gym, the orange-striped cat took such a dislike to their cat.

Suddenly, loud shouting rang out. "I don't care if it cost five hundred dollars! It's not good enough!"

Everyone turned to see Fibby storming

out of the gym and her mother following with a fluffy white cat in a cat carrier.

"But she's a beautiful cat!" Ulna yelled.

"Not as beautiful as Barton's!" Fibby screamed.

With Fibby and her mom gone, people began to look at the other pets again.

"Oh, no!" Leyton cried. "Skinny Kitty is missing!"

"And so is Barton!" said Al-Ian.

CATNAPPED!

To: Catmander Claw on Planet Hiss in
the Feline Galaxy

From: Cat Spy Scratchy on Planet Earth
in the Milky Way Galaxy

Things are fine here on Earth. So far
my presence has gone undetected, and
I continue to take over the minds of
humans and cats. Also, I have met one
really gorgeous Persian Earth cat
babe. Can't wait for you to meet her.

The Tardy Boys and their friends ran to Assistant Principal Snout.

"Our cat's been catnapped!" said Leyton.

The assistant principal raced to the gym's loudspeaker system. "Attention, ladies and gentlemen, we have a report of a catnapping," he announced. "We are going into lockdown. Do not try to leave the gym. Our silver-medalist janitor, Olga Shotput, will now lock the doors."

Olga ran around locking the gym doors.

"Would whoever catnapped the Tardy Boys' cat please return it at once," Assistant Principal Snout announced.

No one moved. Wade whispered something in Snout's ear. "Barton Slugg," the assistant principal said. "Please come forward."

Barton came through the crowd. "Yes, sir?"

"Confidential sources tell me that you may know where the catnapped cat is," said Assistant Principal Snout.

Barton made an innocent face and said, "No, sir."

Assistant Principal Snout turned to the Tardy Boys. "He doesn't know."

"But our cat has to be somewhere in this gym," said Leyton.

"Not if he was catnapped by the Inviso Aliens from Planet C-Thru in the Transparent Galaxy," said Al-Ian.

Wade rolled his eyes and turned to Assistant Principal Snout. "Can't we search everyone?"

"No," said Assistant Principal Snout. "That would violate their right to privacy. Remember, you only *think* your cat was catnapped. It could have run away. Or gotten lost. Or been catnapped by the

Inviso Aliens from Planet C-Thru in the Transparent Galaxy."

"How do you know about the Inviso Aliens?" Al-Ian asked excitedly.

"Everybody knows about the Inviso Aliens," said Assistant Principal Snout.

Wade turned to Leyton and Daisy. "We'll have to look for Skinny Kitty ourselves."

For the next two hours, the Tardy Boys, Al-Ian, and Daisy searched the gym, but they couldn't find Skinny Kitty. Finally, it was time to go. Olga Shotput unlocked the doors, and people put on their heavy winter coats and picked up their pets. The Tardy Boys and their friends stood by the doorway and watched as everyone left.

"Skinny Kitty didn't just disappear," Wade said in a low voice. "Someone in this crowd knows where he is."

Among those leaving was Barton. He was carrying Tinker Bell in her cat carrier and wearing a blue nylon backpack.

"And I still think Barton is the prime suspect," whispered Wade.

"But you heard what Assistant Principal Snout said," said Al-Ian. "We can't search him."

Barton was coming toward them.

"We can't let him get away," Daisy whispered.

"We have to think of something," Wade said.

Leyton tried to think. His tongue stuck out of the corner of his mouth. The monkeys in his head stopped picking fleas off one another and started screeching and swinging from branches. Leyton tried to ignore them and think. But the harder he thought, the louder and more frenzied the monkeys grew!

Meanwhile, Barton was coming closer.

"We have to do something!" Wade hissed.

"But what?" Al-Ian asked.

What? Leyton asked the monkeys swinging around in his skull.

As Barton passed them, he smiled meanly. "Too bad about your cat. I guess he won't get to be in the Catalent Contest after all."

The Catalent Contest, Leyton thought, and the monkeys swung faster and screeched louder. Leyton's brain began to pound. *Thunk!* Suddenly, one of the swinging monkeys in his head slammed into something hard. Leyton wasn't sure what it was or why it was in his head.

Barton was just about to go through the

door when Leyton felt a word come out of his mouth.

And that word was, "Doodley-squat."

Meowrrrooooowwwwwwwlllllll!!!! Something in Barton's backpack suddenly screamed and started to retch and gag. "What the . . ." Barton began to pull off his backpack.

"Gee, Assistant Principal Snout," Wade said loudly. "Sounds like there's a sick cat in Barton's backpack."

Meanwhile, Skinny Kitty kept choking and gagging. Barton frantically opened the backpack. He was just reaching into it when Skinny Kitty went *Blluuuuurrrrpppp!*

"Gross!" Leyton cried.

Daisy reached into Barton's backpack and picked up Skinny Kitty. "There, there," she said, stroking him gently. "It's okay."

Meanwhile, Barton stared in horror at

what Skinny Kitty had left in his backpack.

"How do you think our cat got into your backpack?" Wade asked.

"I have no idea," Barton said.

"That's ridiculous," Leyton said. "Admit you catnapped our cat because you were afraid it had more talent than Tinker Bell."

"Is that true, Barton?" Assistant Principal Snout asked.

"No, sir," said Barton. "My best guess is that this cat must have been tired and crawled into my backpack to get some sleep."

"That sounds reasonable to me," said Assistant Principal Snout.

HISSTORIANS

To: Cat Spy Scratchy on Planet Earth
in the Milky Way Galaxy
From: Catmander Claw on Planet Hiss
in the Feline Galaxy

Our preparations for conquest are now
in their final stages, and we will be
departing for Planet Earth soon. Keep
us informed of your progress. Does
your gorgeous Persian Earth cat babe
have any cute friends?

The next day was Sunday, and the temperature began to drop even more. By Monday, it was so cold that the trees had an icy sheen and kids came to school with their hats pulled down tight and scarves wrapped over their noses and mouths.

After school, the Tardy Boys bundled up and headed to RePete's Cat Palace to get more Nutricat Deluxe. When they got there, they found Daisy outside, marching back and forth with a sign that read

CAGING CATS IS CRUEL

She was shivering, her teeth were chattering, and her lips had turned blue.

"You must be freezing," Wade said. "You better come inside and warm up."

"I c-c-can't," Daisy stammered.

"R-R-RePete d-d-d-doesn't want me in th-th-there."

"He wouldn't want you to freeze," Leyton said, his breath a haze of white mist.

"You b-b-better ask f-f-first," Daisy said.

Wade went inside. RePete was sitting behind the counter. Next to him was a tall silver urn with a small sign that said FREE HOT CHOCOLATE. Beside it was a stack of paper cups.

"Excuse me," Wade said. "Our friend Daisy is outside protesting the way you keep cats in cages. But she's really, really cold and needs to warm up. She could use a cup of hot chocolate. Would you mind letting her come in here for a while?"

RePete frowned. "But she's hurting my business. Why —" he began to say, but then trailed off as he glanced at the orange-striped cat on the pillow behind the counter.

Wade heard soft hissing. Was it his imagination, or were the cat's bright yellow eyes glowing? RePete sat behind the counter without moving or speaking.

"RePete?" Leyton said.

"Huh?" RePete seemed to wake from a daze. His eyes were glassy.

"You started to say that our friend was hurting your business," Wade said.

"No, no, it's fine," RePete said. "Please tell her to come in before she freezes. She can have all the hot chocolate she wants."

That sounded strange to Wade, but he and Leyton got Daisy and brought her inside. When they got to the counter, RePete was pouring steaming cups of hot chocolate. "Here you go."

With trembling hands, Daisy sipped the hot chocolate. "Thank you so much for letting me in. I just want you to know that I'm really not trying to make trouble for you. It's just that I love cats and hate to see them in cages."

"You think those cats upstairs are unhappy?" RePete asked. But as he spoke, the orange-striped cat on the pillow behind the counter stared at Daisy. It hissed, and its bright yellow eyes glowed.

"I can't imagine that any cat in a cage could be —" she began to say, but then trailed off.

"Daisy?" Wade said.

"Huh?" Daisy seemed to wake from a daze. Her eyes looked glassy.

"You started to say that you couldn't imagine that any cat in a cage could be something," Wade said.

Daisy blinked. "I was saying that I can't imagine that any cat in a cage could be . . . er . . . happier than those cats upstairs."

"What?" Leyton said. "Are you sure that's what you meant? I thought you were going to say something completely different."

"I think we better go," Wade said.

"Why?" Leyton asked.

"I just think we should," said Wade.

"But we haven't finished our hot chocolate," said Leyton.

Wade glanced at the orange-striped cat. With a long, low hiss, the cat stared back at him with glowing eyes. Wade began to feel light-headed and dizzy. He tried to look away, but those yellow eyes were like magnets and wouldn't let him go. Suddenly, a voice in Wade's head said, "You will obey my orders."

"No!" Wade cried, tearing his eyes away.

"What?" asked Leyton.

"I won't obey!" Wade staggered away from the counter.

"Won't obey what?" Leyton asked.

Wade didn't want to say anything in front of RePete and the orange-striped cat. "We have to go, Leyton. You, too, Daisy."

"Me?" Daisy asked blankly.

"Yes, you, right now!" Wade pulled her away.

"But what about the Nutricat Deluxe?" Leyton asked.

"You get it," Wade said. "We'll wait for you outside."

Wade and Daisy staggered out into the freezing cold. Tiny white snowflakes had begun to fall from the sky, and Daisy looked up at them.

"Are you okay?" Wade asked.

"Huh?" was all Daisy said.

"Don't you want to protest?" he asked.

"Why?" Daisy asked.

"Because of all those cats in cages," Wade said.

"Cats like being in cages," Daisy said.

"That's not what you said before," said Wade. He picked up the CAGING CATS IS CRUEL sign and showed it to her.

"Where did this come from?" Daisy asked.

"You brought it here," Wade said. "Don't you remember carrying it back and forth in front of the Cat Palace?"

"You must be thinking of someone else," said Daisy.

Leyton came through the doors with a new bag of Nutricat Deluxe.

"Come on," said Wade, taking Daisy's arm. "We have to get out of here."

"Why?" Leyton asked. "What's the rush?"

"Al-Ian's right," said Wade. "There's something seriously weird about that orange-striped cat."

"What makes you say that?" asked Leyton.

"It stared into Daisy's eyes and made her stop protesting the caging of cats," Wade said.

"How do you know the cat did it?" Leyton asked.

"Because then it stared into my eyes and told me to obey its orders," Wade said.

Leyton gave his brother a funny look. "It *spoke* to you?"

"In my mind," Wade tried to explain. "Like it spoke to me with thoughts."

"No way," Leyton said, and turned to Daisy. "You think the orange-striped cat used Alien Space Cat Mind Control on you?"

"There is no such thing as Alien Space Cat Mind Control," Daisy replied. "There are no such things as alien cats. The inhabitants of Planet Hiss in the Feline Galaxy are a friendly race. The Hisstorians are not planning to take over Earth and enslave all humans. The rumors about a surprise attack next Saturday are completely false."

"See?" Leyton said to Wade. "There's no such thing."

Wade stared at his brother in disbelief. "Dude, have you ever heard of Planet Hiss in the Feline Galaxy? Or the Hisstorians?"

"No," said Leyton. "And your point is?"

"How could Daisy know about that stuff

unless that orange-striped cat planted it in her brain?" Wade asked.

"I don't know," said Leyton. "Hey, Daisy, how'd you know about Planet Hiss in the Feline Galaxy and the Hisstorians?"

"There is no such thing as Alien Space Cat Mind Control," Daisy repeated. "There are no such things as alien cats. The inhabitants of Planet Hiss in the Feline Galaxy are a friendly race. The Hisstorians are not planning to take over Earth and enslave all humans. The rumors about a surprise attack next Saturday are completely false."

Wade looked at Leyton and raised an eyebrow as if to say, "See?"

THE
TERRIBLE
TRUTH

To: Catmander Claw on Planet Hiss
   in the Feline Galaxy

From: Cat Spy Scratchy on Planet Earth
   in the Milky Way Galaxy

I have encountered an enemy Purruvian
from Planet Purr. But do not be
concerned. He is thin and weak from
the long journey across space.
When the time comes, I will have

no trouble eliminating him. I have
secretly spread information in the
lamebrain humans that Hisstorians
are a friendly race with no interest
in enslaving any two-legged species.
I have denied all rumors of an
invasion. Believe me, sir, when our
troops attack on Saturday, these
humans will have no idea what hit
them. I asked the gorgeous Persian
Earth cat babe if she has any cute
friends. She said she didn't because
her jerky human owner doesn't let
her play with other cats. Sorry
about that.

The next day was Skating Day. The
Tardy Boys waited for Daisy to come by
their house on the way to the skating
rink, but she didn't show up. Finally, they

left without her. As usual, Al-Ian met them along the way. He was carrying a pair of black ice skates.

"Where are your skates?" he asked the Tardy Boys.

"We'll have to rent some," Wade said.

"Where's Daisy?" asked Al-Ian.

"We think she's under Alien Space Cat Mind Control," said Wade.

Al-Ian's jaw dropped. "So you believe me?"

Wade nodded. "Yesterday I saw it with my own eyes." He told Al-Ian what had happened at RePete's Cat Palace. "That orange-striped cat took control of Daisy's mind and almost got control of mine."

"Did Daisy say anything after the Alien Cat took control of her mind?" Al-Ian asked.

"She just kept repeating the same thing over and over," said Leyton. "'There is no such thing as Alien Space Cat Mind Control. There are no such things as alien cats. The inhabitants of Planet Hiss in the Feline Galaxy are a friendly race. The Hisstorians are not planning to take over Earth and enslave all humans. The rumors about a surprise attack next Saturday are completely false.'"

"Oh, no!" Al-Ian cried. "Do you know what that means? The Hisstorians want to take over Earth and enslave all humans! They're planning a surprise attack next Saturday!"

"No, they're not," said Leyton. "Daisy said the rumors about a surprise attack next Saturday are completely false."

"Leyton, if you were planning a surprise

attack against your enemy, would you want them to know about it ahead of time?" Wade asked.

"No," said Leyton.

"So it makes sense that they want us to think there won't be an attack, right?" said Al-Ian.

"Right," said Leyton.

"And that's how we know they're planning to attack," said Wade.

"Huh?" Leyton still didn't get it.

"It's okay," Wade said. "Just believe us."

"We have to tell someone about the attack," Al-Ian replied.

"Who?" asked Wade.

Suddenly, Al-Ian was struck by the Terrible Truth: *No one in the whole wide world would believe that Earth was going to be attacked by Alien Space Cats!*

"There's no one to tell," said Al-Ian. "Because no one's going to believe us."

"Then what should we do?" asked Leyton.

"There's only one thing we can do," said Wade. "We must stop them ourselves."

THE STRONGEST
FORCE IN
THE UNIVERSE

To: Cat Spy Scratchy on Planet Earth
in the Milky Way Galaxy
From: Catmander Claw Somewhere
in Space

We have launched our ships and are
now on our way to Planet Earth. Make
sure you get rid of that Purruvian.
We expect to arrive on Saturday and

are looking forward to enslaving the humans soon.

At the skating rink, Wade and Leyton carried their rented skates into the changing room. Al-Ian was already there, putting on his skates.

"Have you seen Daisy?" Wade asked.

The words had hardly left his lips when the door to the changing room opened, and Daisy came in. Instead of her long gray coat and roadkill boots, she was wearing a fuzzy pink sweater and matching hat, a plaid wool skirt, and white leggings.

Leyton, Wade, and Al-Ian exchanged puzzled looks. They'd never seen her dressed like that before.

"Hi, Daisy," Wade said. "How are you today?"

"I'm fine, thank you," Daisy replied. But she didn't seem fine to Wade. She seemed like she was still under the spell of Alien Space Cat Mind Control.

"We waited for you at our house this morning," Leyton said.

"Why?" asked Daisy.

"Because you always walk with us," said Wade.

"I do?" asked Daisy, lacing up her skates.

Wade, Leyton, and Al-Ian exchanged a worried look. Daisy was definitely not acting like herself. Just then, Barton Slugg walked in carrying a pair of skates. About a dozen kids were sitting on benches putting on their skates. Barton looked at the kids and then at his feet, which were inside the thick, clear, smell-resistant plastic bags. There was no way he could skate with bags on his feet.

Barton sighed and took the bags off. The kids around him pinched their noses and made sour faces. Barton's toe cheese smelled worse than ever.

"The smell has been concentrated in those bags for days!" Leyton whispered. "Now it's *Extra-Strength*-Toe-Cheese Odor!"

All around the changing room kids quickly began picking up their stuff and leaving. Like everyone else, the Tardy Boys started to get up. The sharp, nasty odor surrounded them, burning their noses and filling their eyes with tears. If they'd been cats, they might have coughed up hair balls. If they'd been hares, they might have coughed up cat balls. Leyton was just about to run out of the room when Wade grabbed him by the shoulder and yanked him back down.

"Why are we staying?" Leyton gasped.

Wade pointed at Daisy, who had just finished tying her skates.

"Achoo!" Suddenly, she sneezed.

"Guhblessyou," said Al-Ian.

Daisy straightened up and blinked. Her forehead furrowed, and she glanced around the changing room as if she wasn't certain where she was. Her eyes looked clear and bright. Then she stared down at her feet. "Why am I wearing ice skates?" she asked out loud.

"Daisy, is that really you?" Wade asked.

"Who else would it be?" she asked. "What's going on? What's that horrible smell? Why am I wearing these strange clothes?"

Wade jumped up and grabbed Daisy by the arm. "Let's get out of here!"

The Tardy Boys and their friends rushed outside where the cold fresh air soothed their burning nostrils.

Wade gave Daisy a hopeful look. "What's the last thing you remember?"

Daisy scowled. "The last thing I remember is . . . sipping hot chocolate at RePete's Cat Palace and that orange-striped cat stared at me and . . . What's going on?"

"We're saved!" Al-Ian cried happily. "The one force in the universe stronger than Alien Space Cat Mind Control is the smell of Barton Slugg's toe cheese!"

"What are you talking about?" Daisy asked.

"That orange-striped cat is no ordinary cat," Al-Ian said. "It's an Alien Space Cat and it used Alien Space Cat Mind Control on you."

Daisy grinned. "That's a good one, Al-Ian."

"I'm serious!" Al-Ian insisted.

Daisy glanced at Wade and Leyton. Both nodded gravely. "It's true," said Wade.

"Not only that," said Al-Ian, "but tomorrow's Saturday, and the Hisstorians are planning to attack Earth!"

TOE FLOSS

To: Catmander Claw Somewhere in Space
From: Cat Spy Scratchy on Planet Earth
in the Milky Way Galaxy

Sir, I have now taken over many human
and cat minds. The Earth cats are
looking forward to enslaving the
humans. It seems that humans have a
very annoying habit of trying to pet
Earth cats when they do not wish to

be petted and Earth cats want that
to stop. Some humans even insist on
having cats declawed! Many declawed
cats are eager to have their humans
defingernailed. I have promised that
we will help them do this. I will
eliminate that Purruvian bag of bones
today. See you soon!

The next morning, the Tardy Boys put
Skinny Kitty in the tattered old backpack
and met Daisy and Al-Ian outside. They
started toward RePete's for the Catalent
Contest, but when they got to the Cat
Palace, the door was locked and the lights
were off.

"Where is everybody?" Leyton asked.

"Maybe we're too late!" Al-Ian said.

"What if the Hisstorians have already attacked and taken over?"

"No, wait," said Daisy, "there's a note on the door."

DUE TO HEAVY TURNOUT
TODAY'S CATALENT CONTEST
HAS BEEN MOVED TO THE GYM
AT THE SCHOOL WITH NO NAME

As they hurried toward The School With No Name, Leyton thought he heard a faint humming sound from above. "Look!" he pointed at the blue sky. High above them were dozens of tiny white streaks.

"It's the Hisstorians in Alien Space Catships!" Al-Ian cried.

"We've got to get to the gym before they do!" Wade yelled.

They ran to The School With No Name.

The parking lot was overflowing with cars.

"There must be hundreds of people inside," Daisy said.

"I bet it's part of the Hisstorians' plan to gather everyone in one place!" Al-Ian realized. They raced through the school entrance and down the hall to the gym. Leyton was just about to push open the door when Al-Ian breathed the word, "Stop!"

"Why?" Wade asked.

"What do you hear?" Al-Ian whispered.

"Nothing," replied Daisy.

"Exactly," whispered Al-Ian. "The parking lot is overflowing with cars. There must be hundreds of people in there, and we don't hear a thing."

"Something weird is going on," Wade realized.

They opened the door just a crack and peeked inside. Hundreds of glassy-eyed men, women, and children stood in rows. Meanwhile, dozens of cats sat in a circle around the orange-striped cat, which stared at them with its glowing yellow eyes and hissed.

"Close the door before they see us!" Daisy whispered.

Al-Ian closed the door. "We're too late!"

"They're all under the spell of Alien Space Cat Mind Control," Wade whispered.

"And it looked like the orange-striped cat was teaching the other cats how to do it!" said Al-Ian. "Once they've learned Alien Space Cat Mind Control, they'll spread out and take over the world!"

"How can we stop them?" Leyton asked.

"We have to get to Barton's feet and

release the terrible smell of his toe cheese," Al-Ian said.

"Whoever does it is going to have to get face-to-face with those feet," Wade warned.

"I think you mean face-to-feet with those feet," said Leyton. "Or more like nose-to-feet. Or really, nose-to-toes."

"Whatever!" Wade snapped impatiently.

"Wait," said Daisy. "If the orange-striped cat is teaching the other cats to use Alien Space Cat Mind Control, won't they all try to stop us?"

"She's right," Wade said. "We'll have to create a diversion."

"No, Wade," Leyton said. "This is a bad time to create a diversion. Right now we have to stop the Alien Space Cats. If you want to create a diversion, you should wait until art class."

Wade groaned and shook his head.

"Here's what we'll do," said Al-Ian. "Three of us will go in and run to the far side of the gym. The cats will follow and try to use Alien Space Cat Mind Control to stop us. Meanwhile, the fourth will sneak over to Barton and take the bags off his feet."

"Who's going to do that?" Leyton asked.

"It should be the strongest and fastest one among us," Al-Ian said.

Everyone looked at Leyton.

"That means you," Wade said.

"But then I'll have to go nose-to-toes with Barton's feet, and my nose will shrivel up and fall off my face," Leyton complained.

"Don't you understand how important this is?" Al-Ian asked. "The fate of the Earth and all of mankind rests on your shoulders."

"So?" said Leyton.

Wade put his hand on his brother's shoulder and led him off to the side where Daisy and Al-Ian couldn't hear. "Maybe you don't care about the fate of the Earth and all of mankind," Wade whispered, "but I don't think you want people to know you've been eating Nutricat Deluxe cat food."

Leyton's eyes widened and his jaw dropped. "You knew?"

"There was no way that little cat could eat all that food," Wade said. "Besides, you always have cat food breath."

"If only I'd followed Assistant Principal Snout's oral hygiene rules," Leyton muttered.

"Too late," said Wade. "So what'll it be? Do I tell everyone you eat cat food? Or do you save the Earth and all of mankind?"

Leyton thought about it. The monkeys in his head started to screech and swing through the trees. They banged their fists against their chests and did backflips. Suddenly, Leyton knew what he had to do.

"I guess I'll save the Earth," he said.

"Good boy." Wade clapped him on the shoulder and led him back to the others.

"Leyton, you wait while we go in and get the cats' attention," Al-Ian said. "Then head for Barton and release the toe cheese odor."

Al-Ian, Daisy, and Wade went into the gym and all the cats ran after them. Then Leyton went in and quietly sprinted toward Barton. Like the other humans, Barton stood motionless, his eyes glassy. Leyton knelt down and reached for the bags on Barton's feet.

But there were no bags!

Leyton didn't understand. Without the bags covering Barton's feet, the terrible odor of toe cheese should have been everywhere. Leyton looked at the floor around Barton, but there was no trail of slime! He strained his brain to understand what was going on. In the vast open spaces inside his head, the monkeys swung from vines and screeched. Then Leyton noticed a piece of white string coming out of one of Barton's shoes. He looked more carefully and saw that something was written on the string in tiny blue letters. It said DR. YANKUM'S TOE FLOSS.

Barton had flossed his toes! This was terrible! Without his horrible toe cheese odor there was no stopping the Hisstorians from taking over the Earth!

Hissssssssss!

Suddenly, Leyton realized he was not alone. He looked up and found himself surrounded by dozens of cats. And they were all staring at him with glowing eyes!

THE END
(IS NEAR)

To: Cat Spy Scratchy on Planet Earth
in the Milky Way Galaxy
From: Catmander Claw Near Earth

Our ships have just entered Earth's
atmosphere and will land in the field
behind The School With No Name. See
you soon!

Surrounded by cats with glowing eyes, Leyton looked for Wade, Daisy, and Al-Ian. Oh, no! They were standing in line with the other glassy-eyed humans. His brother and closest friends had been captured! Leyton swallowed nervously. Now there was only one person left on Earth who knew how to stop the Hisstorians from conquering the entire planet!

And that person wasn't Arnold Schwarzenegger.

It wasn't Spiderman.

It wasn't even Garden Slug Man!

That person was ... Leyton Tardy!

Meanwhile, the glowing eyes of the cats around him sent Alien Space Cat Mind Control Rays at Leyton.

The monkeys in Leyton's head stopped swinging.

They listened to the cats' hissing.

They looked at the cats' glowing eyes.

They felt the Alien Space Cat Mind Control Rays.

Then they looked at one another.

They grinned.

Then they started swinging and screeching again.

What the Alien Space Cats didn't know was that Alien Space Cat Mind Control had two weaknesses: 1) It did not work in the presence of Barton Slugg's toe cheese odor, and 2) It only worked on cats and humans whose skulls were filled with brain cells. Thanks to vast empty spaces in Leyton's skull, Alien Space Cat Mind Control didn't work on him.

But what could one Tardy Boy do against an entire invading force of Alien Space Cats that had the power to take over the Earth? After all, Leyton was just a boy. A simple boy who loved cartoons, empty cardboard boxes, and Nutricat Deluxe cat food. He was not a superhero. He was not a brainiac.

And yet, the future of the Earth and all of mankind now rested on his shoulders.

How, he wondered, *can I possibly overcome such terrible odds?*

The monkeys in his head swung harder and screeched louder. They did backflips and somersaults. They scratched their armpits and bounced off the inside of Leyton's skull. They hung upside down by their tails.

And slowly but surely, for only the

second time in this book and the third time in this (very short) series, an idea appeared.

Suddenly, Leyton knew what he had to do!

(ONLY TWO
CHAPTERS
UNTIL)
THE END

To: Catmander Claw Landing in the Field
Behind The School With No Name
From: Cat Spy Scratchy in the Gym

Preparations are complete. Planet
Earth is ready to be conquered!

Leyton raced toward the boys' locker room. Inside, he held his breath and went to the one place where he'd never been before — the Aisle of Death. It was like a ghost town. Dust covered the bench. The lockers were open and empty. No one — not even silver-medal-winning janitor Olga Shotput — dared to come here. Leyton's eyes began to water. He held his nose tightly to keep it from jumping off his face and running away. The lockers closest to Barton's were bent because the toe cheese odor was so strong it had weakened the metal and peeled the paint.

Leyton's heart pounded and his lungs hurt. He needed to breathe, but he knew that if he dared open his mouth this close to THE MOTHER OF ALL TOE CHEESES, it would be his last breath ever!

With trembling hands, he opened Barton's locker. Lying on the bottom was a greasy-looking gray thing that might have once been a sock. Leyton grabbed a badminton racket lying on the bench and slid it under the greasy-looking gray thing. It felt heavier than a normal sock because it was filled with trillions of fat, happy toe cheese bacteria.

Carrying the badminton racket upon which lay the greasy-looking gray thing that might have once been a sock, Leyton ran down the hall. Suddenly, a loud roar came from outside, and the floor under his feet began to shake. Through the window, he saw that the snow in the field behind the gym was being blown into the air so hard it formed a thick cloud. And yet it was a calm, windless day and, in other places, the snow lay undisturbed like a peaceful white blanket.

Leyton didn't have time to wonder what was causing the roaring and shaking. He had to get to the gym. It wasn't that he was so eager to save the Earth and all of mankind, but if he didn't get rid of the greasy-looking gray thing that might have once been a sock, the fat, happy toe cheese bacteria might crawl down the neck of the badminton racket and cause his fingernails to fall off!

"Stop!" Olga Shotput blocked the hall. In her hands was her trusty broom. "Where are you going with that disgusting, smelly thing?"

"I have to get to the gym before it's too late," Leyton said.

"Too late for what?" asked Olga.

"Too late to stop the attack of the Alien Space Cats," said Leyton.

"And leave that disgusting thing for me to clean up?" Olga said.

"But I'm talking about saving the Earth and all of mankind," Leyton said.

"Oh, sure," said Olga. "And who'll get all the credit for saving them? You! Meanwhile, I'll get stuck cleaning up the mess."

"No, no!" Leyton said. "I promise you'll get credit for saving them, too."

"You expect me to believe that?" Olga chuckled bitterly. "They told me there was a Spring Olympics, and I believed them! They told me I'd win a gold medal in custodianship, and I believed them! But that was the end! I'm finished with the lies."

"But I swear," Leyton insisted. "Just let me get to the gym, and we'll be able to save everyone!"

"Over my dead body!" Olga growled, and held the broom out like a weapon.

Leyton tried to get around her. He faked right and went left, but Olga blocked him with the broom. He faked left and went right, but Olga was there! Leyton faked up and went down. He faked down and went up. He faked in and went out. He faked out and went in. It was no use. No matter how he tried, he couldn't get past her!

Meanwhile, the fate of the Earth and all of mankind hung by a thread!

"Meow."

Olga looked down. Skinny Kitty rubbed itself against her leg and purred. He looked up and his green eyes twinkled.

Olga blinked and became still.

Skinny Kitty looked at Leyton. Once again his green eyes twinkled. A little voice in Leyton's head said, "What are you waiting for? Go save the Earth and all of mankind."

Leyton ran into the gym where humans stood in rows, waiting for orders from the Alien Space Cats. The orange-striped cat was hissing at all the other cats. Sitting next to him was Tinker Bell. Leyton raced up and down the rows, waving the greasy-looking gray thing that might have once been a sock under people's noses and spreading the awful, nose-burning odor throughout the gym. People began to blink, and their glassy eyes became clear again.

"Where am I?" one of them asked.

"Why are we standing in rows?" asked someone else.

The orange-striped cat hissed loudly and dozens of cats raced toward Leyton. They stared at him with glowing eyes, but the monkeys in Leyton's skull just laughed and continued to pick fleas off one another. Leyton swung the greasy-looking gray thing that might have once been a sock at the cats, and they all hissed and scattered.

By now, most of the people in the gym had woken up from the Alien Space Cat Mind Control. Leyton stopped next to his brother and friends. Wade blinked. "What happened?"

"The whole gym was under Alien Space Cat Mind Control," Leyton said. "But I saved everyone with this." He held up the badminton racket with the greasy-looking gray thing that might have once been a sock.

"Gross!" Wade cried, and staggered backward, holding his nose. "Get that thing away from me!"

"But it saved you!" Leyton said.

"If you don't take it away, it's gonna kill me, too," said Wade.

Suddenly, a scream of grief and agony filled the gym and Barton Slugg shouted, *"Tinker Bell!"*

(THIS WOULD HAVE BEEN) THE END (BUT THE AUTHOR ADDED SOME OTHER STUFF)

To: Catmander Claw in the Field Behind
The School With No Name
From: Cat Spy Scratchy in the Gym

Abort mission! Turn all ships around
and return to Planet Hiss at once!
Humans have developed an antidote
to Alien Space Cat Mind Control!
Don't know how those two-legged
morons did it!

The Tardy Boys and their friends
followed Barton outside. The orange-
striped cat and Tinker Bell bounded
through the snow toward a small orange
space vehicle.

"Tinker Bell, stop!" Barton yelled. "Don't
leave!"

But it was too late. A door opened in the
space vehicle, and the orange-striped cat
and Tinker Bell ran inside. The door
closed. There was a loud roar and a blast
of smoke and snow. The ground shook,
and the space vehicle shot into the sky.

"Tinker Bell!" Barton cried out, and
threw himself face-first onto the snow,
kicking and wailing.

The Tardy Boys and their friends started
back toward the gym. Ahead of them,

dozens of people were leaving with their cats. RePete came out with his empty cat carrier.

Wade said, "Sorry about that orange-striped cat, RePete."

"Why should I repeat that?" RePete asked. "Why does everyone always tell me to repeat?"

"They're not telling you to repeat," Daisy said. "They're saying RePete because that's your name."

"No, it's not," said RePete.

"It's spelled R-E-P-E-T-E," said Daisy.

"Aha!" RePete cried. "Now I understand! You say *repeat* because you think that is how my name is pronounced. But it's not. My name is French. It's pronounced *Ray-Pet-tuh*."

"So who won the Catalent Contest?" Al-Ian asked.

"No one," said RePete. "It's canceled due to the Alien Space Cat attack."

"If the Catalent Contest is canceled, does that mean we can't win a year's worth of Nutricat Deluxe?" asked Leyton.

"Yes," said RePete.

"But how will they afford to feed themselves and Skinny Kitty?" Daisy asked.

Wade glanced at Leyton and then said, "I wouldn't worry, Daisy. From now on, I think Skinny Kitty will be eating less food than he used to."

Back inside the gym, they put Skinny Kitty in his tattered backpack. Silver-medalist janitor Olga Shotput swept the gym floor while Assistant Principal Snout put away the tables.

The Tardy Boys and their friends left The School With No Name and started home. Wade patted Leyton on the back.

"You did it, dude! You saved the Earth and all of mankind!"

"That's right!" Daisy realized. She threw her arms around his neck and gave him a big hug.

"You saved the *entire* Earth!" Al-Ian said. "No one's ever done that before! That makes you THE GREATEST HERO IN HISTORY!"

Leyton beamed. He could have told them that without Skinny Kitty's help he would not have saved the Earth and become THE GREATEST HERO IN HISTORY, but he decided against it. The monkeys in his skull jumped down from their branches and started marching in a parade, waving banners and playing trumpets and banging drums. Leyton decided he really liked being a hero.

They came around a tall snowdrift. Standing before them was someone wearing sunglasses and dressed all in white. The Tardy Boys and their friends stopped.

"Who's that?" Daisy whispered.

"The person who brought Skinny Kitty to us," Wade answered.

"Is it a he or a she?" Al-Ian whispered.

"We're not sure," said Wade.

The person in white pointed at the tattered backpack containing Skinny Kitty and held out his/her hand.

"He/she wants Skinny Kitty!" Al-Ian realized.

Leyton hated to see Skinny Kitty go. On the other hand, if Skinny Kitty went, then Leyton could have the rest of the Nutricat Deluxe to himself. He handed the backpack to the person in white.

The person in white handed Leyton a note and then walked away behind a snowdrift. Leyton unfolded the note.

"What's it say?" Wade asked eagerly.

Dear Sons,

If you are reading this note, it means that you have saved the Earth and all of mankind. We are very proud of you. We have known for several months that the Hisstorians were planning to attack Earth. That skinny tabby cat is not really ours. He is a Purruvian commando cat sent from the Planet Purr to help you stop the Hisstorians from succeeding in their evil plan. We pretended he was our cat because we were worried that if we told you that you had to save the Earth, it might cause you some stress.

We are still being held by alien kidnappers, but they are nice and let us eat pizza and watch reruns of American Idol. We hope you are eating well, getting enough sleep, and getting good grades in school. Watch out for the cuddly glowbunnies.

Love,
Mom and Dad

(JUST PAST)
THE END

If you have ever read a book before, you
may have noticed that some authors put
things called acknowledgments in them.
Acknowledgment is a really big word that
basically means that if you lent the
author money or bought him a nice meal,
he's never going to pay you back. Instead,
he'll pretend that you'll be so happy to
see your name in his book that you'll

never mention the money or food again.

Some authors write long acknowledgments that thank everyone from their parents and editors (usually pretty important people) to the pizza delivery guys (the *really* important people). Other authors use acknowledgments to name lots of famous and rich people so that you (the reader) will know that he (the author) has plenty of rich and famous friends who have probably lent him a lot of money and bought him some really good meals.

You can usually tell how much an author owes a person by how many fancy words he uses. If he just says thank you, then he probably only owes twenty-five dollars. But if he writes that he'll be forever indebted to you for your extraordinary personal support throughout his long, arduous journey, then you've lost at least five hundred dollars.

The author of this book doesn't owe money to any of the people in his acknowledgments (see beginning of book). He doesn't even know any of them. He just likes the food they make. Except for Catherine Zeta-Jones. In her case, the author hopes that if he puts her name in his book she'll go on a date with him.

If you would like to know if Catherine Zeta-Jones went on a date with the author, you'll probably have to read the next book in this series, *Is That a Glow-in-the-Dark Bunny in Your Pillowcase?*, which the author plans to start writing as soon as he finishes his bowl of Nutricat Deluxe with mustard and soy sauce.